Five Days of Dick

randall 'Jay' andrews

JaCol Publishing Inc.

Copyright 2017 by JaCol Publishing Inc.

FIRST PRINTING

February 2017

All rights reserved

JaCol Publishing Inc.

2008 Hoquiam Ave NE

Renton, WA 98059

818-510-2898

ISBN: **978-1-946675-12-5**

JaCol Publishing

Table of Contents

Chapter 1..1

Chapter 2..6

Chapter 3..10

Chapter 4..15

Chapter 5..19

Chapter 6..23

Chapter 7..27

Chapter 8..29

Chapter 9..36

Chapter 10..41

Chapter 11..46

Chapter 12..51

Chapter 13..55

Chapter 14..60

Chapter 15..65

Chapter 16..69

Chapter 17..74

Chapter 18..77

Chapter 19..83

Chapter 20..87

Chapter 21..92

Chapter 22..96

Chapter 23..100

Chapter 24..104

Chapter 25..108

Chapter 26..113

Chapter 27..117

Chapter 28..122

Chapter 29..127

Chapter 30..131

Chapter 31..135

Chapter 32..139

Chapter 33..143
Chapter 34..147
Chapter 35..150
Chapter 36..154
Chapter 37..158
Chapter 38..163
Chapter 39..168
Chapter 40..172
Chapter 41..178
Chapter 42..183
Chapter 43..188
Chapter 44..192
Chapter 45..197
Chapter 46..204
Chapter 47..208
Chapter 48..214
Chapter 49..220
Chapter 50..225
Chapter 51..229
Chapter 52..236

Acknowledgement

I can't begin to thank the wonderful writers who have graced my world. From Writers World, where thousands have come to learn the craft of writing and kick around critiques of their current projects, to the boot camps where writers take a vested interest in finishing manuscripts, they have been inspirational in pushing all of us to publish.

I thank Colleen Ries, who has been my partner in JaCol Publishing and did the groundwork for getting us up and flying. She put her footprint on the company and helped give it the quality we continue to maintain.

I thank those who have come aboard JaCol since then: Kathy Johnson, who plays the best girl Friday, and has been there to see that we don't sink under the demand of jobs beyond my editing: Maggie McGarvey, who has taken over the duties of everything Writers World, and for the small technical duties of formatting. She's been a major cog.

I thank all the artists we work with, and on this one—Katie Ketchum and Karen Brosinsky. Katie does many of my covers, and Karen is there to letter them.

Finally, I thank my family. They have to put up with a writer for a husband and dad.

To those I have regrettably not mentioned, know you aren't forgotten.

Foreword

I met Randall and Dick almost simultaneously.

Having stumbled into the virtual critique group, I found a collection of writers and editors devoted to elevating their own work and edifying others. At the center of it all, Randall wields his editor's pen with precision, culling passive verbs, overwritten phrases, and awkward construction.

A firm believer in "show don't tell," Randall offers his own work as perfect examples of how to construct everything from personal essays to character studies. His exposition and descriptions never fail to disappoint.

When he shared the first chapters of *Five Days of Dick* with me, Randall prefaced it by saying, "this one's for everyone who says curse words don't belong in quality writing."

True to form every word in this delightful romp is right on point. Equal parts comedy and noir, Dick Dillard's curmudgeon of an antihero takes the reader on a fast-paced journey through murder, intrigue, and just the right amount of sex.

Enjoy the ride; I know you'll love Dick as much as I do.

-Maggie McGarvey

Chapter 1

If you think this is going to be a pleasant novel, you might want to leave now; if you trust me when I say prepare for a bumpy ride, you should strap in. Everything I'm going to discuss about my life is nothing more than the culmination of shit I've had to deal with for nearly fifty years. From the idea Christ is out there waiting for me to be a better person, to the dumb cunt who finished off my innocence by licking my nuts, I don't want you left in the dark on what I think–about anything.

I liked being me, the guy who said, "Yeah, whatever," every time I had to confront some dickhead who had an opinion I didn't agree with. However, some brilliant asshole decided I should become a writer, and you have to play nice if you want a readership beyond your mom and dad. After that, someone else granted me permission to offer up advice on what writers should do to make their slop more palatable to the krill of readers out there. Thankfully, that didn't require I play nice.

My question for 90% of the garbage I pick up is, "Why the fuck can't you emote?" Like I give a shit if your vampire sways in the breeze, your werewolf has bloodshot eyes, or your romance novel has some fireman chiseled like Adonis. If that's all you have, maybe you shouldn't give up that day job at Walmart. The novel isn't in you and they're missing someone asking customers to "Please come back again."

The reality is that visceral is universal; it touches our soul. If you can plunge the knife in so deep it makes me bleed, or causes tears to roll down my face, you can go far, but if you think it doesn't take talent, and you might be the next Stephanie Meyer, guess what? Shitty writers who make it big come around very seldom, and our allotment of Meyer and James is taken. The fact that those two hacks stumbled and fell into a pile of shit good fortune doesn't mean you will. It's called Power Ball and you have a better chance of winning that than writing the million dollar novel.

God damn, my mood has turned shitty.

All because I tossed and turned thinking about how my dumb-cunt ex wife left me for the first douche bag who promised her more than I could. Not that I cared; however, that dipshit attorney of hers sure sent me over the edge.

I woke up five days ago, and like every morning for the past ten years since she left, I grabbed my coffee from the local pee-hole gas station, put twenty down and asked for the rest on pump four. Of course, I couldn't keep the coffee upright and spilled half of it down my shirt.

I don't have to tell you the style or color of the shirt—it doesn't help the fucking story. Maybe you should figure that out too.

Anyway, when I made it to my office, some dumb bitch had left half a dozen messages on my machine about her displeasure with my review of her work, as though proving her inability to take criticism would make her more endearing, and wanted me to take back what I wrote in that generic 'not this time' letter. "Sorry Mrs. Howard, but Dillard Publishing won't be using your manuscript at this time, blah, blah, blah."

Mrs. Howard felt something entirely different about her work, and by God, she planned to make sure I sucked it up like a toothless senior citizen. I was her hack, I had no business reading her fine work, work her family told her read like the best damn shit they'd ever laid eyes on, which, my guess amounted to the comic section of the Sunday paper. Her rant amazed me. I couldn't get enough of it, and after playing it back, over and over like my favorite song, lo and behold, she called again.

"Hello?" I put on my pretty face.

"Is Mr. Dillard there?" Her tone sharpened.

"Speaking."

"How the fuck…" The rest spilled out in an incoherent rant, pretty much like her manuscript. As much as I wanted to debate the merits of her work, I knew she intended to talk over me, and anything I said she wouldn't listened to, so I put the receiver on the table and sipped my coffee, offering every once in awhile an audible "Uh huh." As long as I could hear the drone of her voice, I figured I was pretty safe.

After fifteen minutes, she exhausted herself, and I slipped in "Are you through?"

In between her sniveling, she tried to work me for a second chance. "Please, Mr. Dillard, can't you take another look?"

My fingers already had. I lit up my computer screen and scrolled through her over dramatized crap, a romance novel with so many clichés it would have astounded me if any fucking took place at all. I tried to figure out how to reverse her bipolar anxiety and keep her on the good side of life, while letting her know this novel was best read between the cheeks of her ass as she used it for toilet paper. It wasn't going to happen. This turned into one of those moments where nothing short of "I will give you a million dollars for your work" would placate her.

I'd had enough. "Mrs. Howard, let's be real, it isn't very good."

"Why?" I put it in a question, but in reality, I should have used an exclamation point because she didn't ask a question when she blurted, "Why." It was code for "Fuck you."

She had a character whose husband had cheated on her with the "Gorgeously sophisticated and attractive next door neighbor, Raquel, who always dressed in silky white negligees that hung to her knees, whose breast were as plastic as legos and as rock hard as over-baked dinner rolls. She had legs so long they reached her shoulders, and she smelled as though she bathed in perfume." I couldn't wrap my mind around that overwritten description, but apparently her family could. So her protagonists went on a hedonistic romp of one sexual encounter after another; first the mailman, then the pool boy, followed by a chance encounter with a police officer looking for a dog—along with a fireman. The sheer believability underwhelmed me; however, the necessity for a plot left me wanting. "I"ll tell you why!" I blurted over the phone.

Dead silence, and it felt golden.

"Did this shit happen to you?" I suspected her husband divorced her; clearly she had issues with someone.

She returned with a meek response, "The cheating part did."

"And did you start fucking everything that moved, Mrs. Howard?"

In a moment of clarity, she emoted something I could grab a hold of. "I wanted to."

"Exactly, you wanted to. I bet you felt pretty shitty that your husband left you for some bimbo who probably looked a lot prettier and younger than you, and I'm sure a hell of a lot more fun."

"How dare you, Mr. Dillard."

I cut her off. "No, how dare you. How dare you lie to your readers. Admit it, you fired up the Jim Dandy and plugged that hole of yours every night for a year, imagining all the men who loved your kooch. You cried yourself to sleep with a dose of disappointment and a barrel of shame. That's what really happened, and the truth is, that's what your readers want to hear. It's how they feel. They want to hear what fucked up thoughts you had and how you overcame them, because they have them too! How about writing about that, Mrs. Howard? How about telling your readers how you can overcome your shitty life by keeping a journal of your shitty life."

She responded with the calm of a doldrums, "I can see we are done talking, Mr. Dillard."

"Sadly, I guess we are." I wanted to tell her to take my advice, but she hung up before my final word drew air. That's how the last five days began, and guess what, that was just the beginning.

Chapter 2

I had an office in the Picamore district of downtown, a retro second-story brick-walled room with a half moon window overlooking a refurbished promenade. Down below, pretty twenty somethings dined at boutique outdoor cafes, and busy thirty somethings hiked up their power skirts to sit like men. A mosaic of the new cool, and in truth, it was cool. So, there I sat in a top-of-the-world office space when Michaels, the property manager dropped by with some over-tanned, pinstriped attorney asking all sorts of questions about how long I planned on occupying my lease, as though I had some other place more suited to my lifestyle as a dinosaur publisher. I could see the attorney drooling, hot for my space, standing at the window and ogling over the bouncing tits below. I could imagine him with the shades down, that one miscued slat where he's peering through, his pants down to his knees, and him rubbing one out to the tune of the beauties below.

"I'm fine, Hal. I don't see me leaving anytime soon."

The attorney swung around from the window and thrust his hand out. "Jim, Jim Hunter. I would be willing to pay you to break the lease."

I looked at his hand with disdain. "Oh, you would? How much are we talking?" Not that I really gave a shit, but I wanted to hear his offer.

"Well, Mr. Dillard, I would be willing to give you an even five thousand."

That little fuck.

It moved me to overdrive. "Five thousand! My goodness, I could go far with that."

Hal cut to the chase. "How much then?"

I turned to Michaels. "More than you would give me, Hal. I've been here nearly twenty years, back when your father ran this property, back when I looked down on junkies and hookers..." not that most of those there now weren't anything more than glorified junkies and hookers... "and I gave your dad better than the going rate, and some great advice, advice that led to the promenade. So, if you don't mind, I don't have a figure below seven digits. You up for that?"

He remained motionless, but his young attorney suitor chuckled. "Well Hal, maybe you should tell him what our plans are for this building?"

"Our plans? Are you a business partner, Jim, Jim Hunter?"

"No, I'm not but—"

"Then shut the fuck up. As though you have jack shit to say about what is done around here."

He held his ground. "Well, Mr. Dillard, like you, I have made suggestions as to what the next phase of this renovation should be, and quite frankly, it doesn't include low traffic businesses like low volume publishers."

I smiled, because for an attorney, he wasn't too up on the reality of my lease. "So, you think that you're going to make this building a high traffic building, is that it? Sort of make the commercial space up here as heavy in volume as down below?"

He verbally took a swing at me, "That and a higher clientele of patrons."

"Oh, so writers are a pretty shady lot are they?"

He raised his eyebrows in agreement, and I realized he was much younger than he first appeared. I had guessed his age as mid thirties, but on closer examination, especially around the eyes, he looked more like mid twenties. "Hal, you are going to listen to this pup?"

Jim took exception and thumped his chest. "This pup is a partner in Hunter and Hunter."

"Are you one of those Hunters?"

"When they add another Hunter I will be."

"Let me guess, dad and granddad?" I sat on the edge of my desk, crossed my arms and tilted my head in speculation.

"As a matter of fact." He acted nearly as arrogant as he did a dipshit.

"As a matter of fact?"

Smug little prick.

He insisted. "That's right."

"Any other Hunters who practice?"

"My sister will be a partner when she passes the bar." He put his arms akimbo and barely stared eye level with me, and I sat on my desk.

"Well, so when your sister climbs aboard have you considered changing your signage to a green four leaf clover with an H on each leaf?"

Hal snickered and Jim questioned, "What?"

"The four H club, you turd. Now, go away, I have writers to harass."

He continued, "So I am to assume you have no intentions of considering an offer?"

I circled around to my seat, sat in comfortably and swiveled with my back to them. "Apparently you haven't read my lease agreement, something that was written by Hal's father, have you?"

I could hear him whispering. "What's he talking about?"

"Good day, gentlemen." I swung around as they walked away. "Jim?"

He stopped and turned. "Yes?"

"Does your sister look anything like you?"

"Some would say yes."

"Send her up next time. You'd make a damn fine looking woman. I want to see that."

They rattled my door as they shut it behind them.

Chapter 3

I returned to the pile of shithole submissions on my desk, a stack of manila envelopes from various corners of the globe. Writers who probably exhausted the bigger houses and found my name in the Writers Guide under the "When all else fails, try them" section. I often wound up acquiring rejects; sort of the story of my life. If I didn't acquire reject writers, I acquired reject women, women who made the last stop on crazy train. From my first girlfriend in grade school, to my former wife, Muffin, I attracted women who had a one way ticket to Bedlam Asylum, women who if they had nothing horrible to say said nothing at all. I know I'm to blame, because I am a slave to pussy. I'm willing to overlook the flaws, like no personality, unstable, antisocial, unhinged at the slightest disappointing news, for their desire to screw like rabbits.

I read four or five submission letters without reaching it to the 'thank you.' If you can't write a query, I'm not going to read your three retarded, illegible chapters. Before I knew it, I'd carefully signed five rejection letters and licked the SASE envelopes for my noon mail call. However, when I picked up the sixth query, the opening line struck me. "I'm a whore, and is that so bad?"

Do tell.

"My exploits aren't one of pride but of necessity, and it is with regret that I admit to being a bit of a masochist, or perhaps a sadist. Either way, the end results never benefit anyone involved."

I couldn't make out if this woman wrote a fictional piece or a memoir, she hadn't said. Not your typical fare for a letter, but what the hell, it intrigued me. She had clean, crisp writing that flowed. I pulled out her sample chapters and a photo tumbled to the desk. If she wrote fiction, I wondered if the photo was the author's take on what the character should look like. If the photo was the author, she drew me in—late thirties or a well kept forty. She turned sideways with a grand shot of her upper body, breasts heaving forward in a thin shirt that nipples protruded through, her face to the camera as though caught by surprise, as though I had captured her. She stared into the eye of the camera, directly at me. Fuck, she compelled me, aroused me, intrigued me, and I knew I had to find out more. Whoever this woman was, she had my attention, and the only way I would turn off my thoughts would be if her manuscript read like the biggest pile of dog shit. I planned to give her the benefit of the doubt for at least ten pages.

It didn't take ten pages. It didn't take two pages. It didn't take two sentences. Her opening had me. "My name's Deloris, and without knowing who you are, I want you." She followed it up by building on that sentence, by drawing the reader into her world of what she planned to do, or what she had already done. I devoured the first chapter, then the second. When the mailman came by, I shouted, "Come back fucking later!" Be damned with the rejection letters, those authors knew they were shitty; they could wait another day for me to tell them so.

As if my mystery author watched me, my phone rang, and a sultry voice asked me if I had discovered a manuscript from D. Hallorin. I rifled through the stack to find the manuscript's envelope. HALLORIN. "Yes, I am reading it now."

"Oh, are you the publisher or the editor?"

That made me laugh. I did everything; the janitor, maid, and ass wiper. "Both."

"Do you think it's good enough to be published?"

Having made it through the first two and half chapters, I had enough sense to admit, "I haven't read enough to make that determination." I added, "But what I've read so far, it's well written."

She sounded disappointed. "Oh."

"That's a good thing, Ms. Hallorin."

Her voice echoed through the receiver, "Please, call me Dee."

Intrigued, I continued. "Dee, can I ask a question?"

She read me like a book. "Is the story fiction?"

"Yes."

"I think so, but perhaps not as much as I'd like to admit."

That gave me an erection. I don't know if her voice or the fact this author toyed with me about being the woman in the pages did it, but if I was Jim, Jim Hunter the attorney, I would have whipped my cock out and started playing with it. Instead, I imagined her naked body standing in my doorway around midnight with a 'fuck me' look on her face.

Of course, who was I kidding? From the picture, she had enough sense not to saddle up with the likes of me. I had slipped into one of my assorted daily fantasies. I'd let myself go and wasn't the prettiest of boys anymore, or for that matter, ever was. My one redeeming quality, my no nonsense attitude, flattened into acerbic rants against my fellow man. The last time I laid someone, she bartended at my local watering hole and had the name of a horse— Trudy. I had been too drunk to make my way home, so she took me upstairs to her apartment and apparently screwed my brains out. I didn't remember any of it, and from the mileage on Trudy, that might have been a good thing.

I looked for an address on the envelope, only the town appeared—this town. "How many publishers have you submitted your work to?"

She went silent before informing me, "You are the only one."

"Why me?"

"Honestly?"

"Please."

"Well, I don't have a lot of cash to send sample manuscripts to a bunch of publishers, only to get rejected. I didn't even mail that to you, I dropped it off in your mail slot."

I looked at the envelope, no stamps. She didn't have a SASE, or a return address, just her name D. Hallorin, and the town. "If I like this, how would I have gotten a hold of you?"

She laughed. "Why do you think I'm calling you?"

I wanted to believe there was more to it, that she'd wanted me from afar, but I had enough smarts to know better. "So if I like it, will you send me the rest of the manuscript?"

"Could I drop it off instead?"

My prick told me, God damn right she could. "Let me finish reading the rest. Do you have a number where I can reach you?"

"When do you think you will be done reading the chapters I sent?"

I thumbed through the rest of it. "An hour."

"I'll call back then." She hung up. No thank you, no goodbye, just a click.

I finished the work. I felt like she played me. It had to be plagiarized; it read too damn well to be from a first time author. I took some key lines and googled them, but nothing came up. I twiddled my thumbs wondering why this woman wasn't plastered all over the Times Best Seller List. I wanted more of her writing. I couldn't wait for an hour to pass. When it did—no call. I waited some more. No call. Four o'clock rolled around, and I still hadn't heard from the mysterious author of the work sitting in front of me, work better than any manuscript I'd read in my twenty-plus years in the business.

I rubbed my face in disappointment. She wasn't calling. Out the window, the promenade tower, a four-faced clock, rolled around to five, and I hadn't done anything productive other than know this woman was someone I wanted to publish, or maybe her story transfixed me, maybe her picture had a hold of my balls. I didn't know; I knew I had to read more.

Chapter 4

I stood and lifted my coat off the rack, exiting to a gentle breeze running from one hallway open window to the other. I turned, locked the door and noticed a slip of paper taped to it. I leaned in and read:

"Dear Mr. Dillard, I have second thoughts. I doubt this work is worth your time. Thank you for entertaining a foolish woman and her dream of dreaming big."

"Fuck me!" My voice echoed down the hall. She must have been a dormouse. I usually heard all the floor boards creak when someone crossed my door. I yanked the paper off and turned it over, hoping to find some sort of clue about my mystery woman. The flip side was a receipt for coffee lattes at the deli downstairs.

I made my hibernating crawl out of my office, something I seldom did this early in the day, and found myself standing in a line of after-work debutantes, musing about the misfortunes of toiling in a male dominated society. The pair in front of me jockeyed over Darryl, the resident lizard in their office, and who had the better story of his lecherous come-ons. I gathered he was a boss by their descriptions. Trust me, when they figured out their promotion sat at the end of his cock, they'd be fighting to plant their panty-less butt up on the copy machine.

Get on with it, ladies, I have questions!

When I arrived front center of my barista, a kid so unhappy to be there, he recited in a shallow peep that poured from his lips in a monotone lacquer, "Welcome to The Coffee Pot, can I help you?" He didn't look up and had a "wish I could kill every motherfucker in here" trance about him.

I slid the photo of the woman under his gaze. "Did you see this woman today?"

He lifted the image closer to his face. "Dude, I see people all day long, most of which I wish I didn't. I can't tell you one face from another."

I pulled out a ten. "Does this refresh your memory?"

He said, "If you want it to." he palmed the bill against the glass and started to slide it to him.

I put my hand over his. "Did you see her?"

"She comes in all the time. Sits over there." He pointed to a round table tucked away in the far corner. "Writes on a computer and drinks iced mocha lattes."

I studied the receipt, a tab for six iced mocha lattes. "Thanks."

"So are you tipping me or not?" We both had half ownership on the bill held tightly against the counter.

I released it and asked, "Is she here every day?"

"Usually, but it's weird, for a woman who never speaks, she made it a point to tell me a man was going to come in looking for her, and to tell him that she wouldn't be coming in for a few weeks, but she would be around."

Un-fucking believable.

She played cat and mouse with me. What was her angle? "Give me an iced mocha latte."

He acted dejected, as though it was coming out of the ten. "Don't worry, keep the ten." I handed him another bill.

I took my drink over to the desk where she usually sat; a young woman put her things down. "Excuse me, may I have this spot?" There weren't any other tables open.

"Uh, no. I found this first."

I pulled another ten out. "I'll buy the spot."

She looked around. "Seriously?"

I bowed my head. "It's important."

She sighed as though helping another male was the story of her life, a life she appeared unhappy with. "Fine, and you can keep your ten," as if accepting it meant I wanted a blow job.

"Young lady, not all pay it forwards are with caveats."

"What?" She tilted her head as though I had a foreign tongue.

"I appreciate your understanding." I tucked the bill between the cover of two books. "Thank you."

She didn't resist and walked to the outdoor tables.

I positioned myself in the chair my mystery writer sat in when she typed, able to view the entire joint, outside promenade as well. "What is it about this seat that you value?" I sipped on her brand of coffee, getting into her state of mind. The promenade had a water fountain in the center, and from her spot you had a spectacular view of water dancing in the air, spinning and arcing, glistening in the sun. When the peaks rested, across the grounds you had a view of the Cineplex, all the movie titles strung across the marquee. The signage drew me in, much as I suppose anyone who looked at the multitude of bulbs, blinking a rhythm, would be. I bet you watch at least one movie a week. I didn't much care for the chocolate; I think it's a chick thing, or at least a sweet addiction. I liked my shit black, period.

So she wasn't going to be there for awhile, but she would be around. I wondered why. Maybe she wanted a constant view of the marquee, maybe the dancing water wore on her. Or maybe, she wanted a view of this seat I sat in.

Chapter 5

Twenty-four hours can calm seas or bend cocks, and in my case, I needed the latter. I found myself back at my desk without a gawd damn thing other than my mysterious Ms. Hallorin on my mind. I didn't sleep well, I never did, but something about her words on the page and sound of her voice drew me to her flame. Being a moth didn't sit well, but fuck it, it beat drinking coffee all day and reading work a junior high English teacher would reject. I snapped up the pile of submissions from that day's cattle call and shoved them into my briefcase. The coffee shop had a table waiting for me.

I made it downstairs and found a ten-year old sitting at my spot, her mother behind me in line. With my chocolate latte in hand, I plopped my bag on the table and sat across from the waif.

"Excuse me, mister, but this table is for my mommy and me."

"Scram, kid."

She pursed her lips, squinted, and crossed her arms in defiance. "I'm not going anywhere."

"Suit yourself."

My work absorbed most the table. I spread out submissions into three piles: Shitty, shittier, and shittiest. The first victim had a handful of red marks when the child's mother made it to the table.

"Um, I think you have our table."

"Look, no offense, but either you can pull a chair up and join me, or you can—" I scanned the room, not an empty table inside or out, "find another spot."

Her indignation splayed across her face like a gutted chicken. "What?"

"You heard me."

"You are an asshole."

I winked, lifted my wallet from my pocket and pulled out a ten. "That I am, but I pay to be that way." I slid the bill to her. "I apologize, I'm observing something from this spot and it's sort of important. I promise you, if you wish to stay, you won't hear a peep from me."

For all her bravado, she shrugged okay and borrowed a chair. In the corner of the coffee shop, around a circular table, those two sat opposite me, carrying on about stupid shit moms and ten-year-old girls talk about. I had promised to stay mute, but at that point when the little girl's mom said, "Honey, don't point out a man's flaws until you have your hooks in him," I cried, "Bullshit."

"I'm sorry, but could you please not use that language around my child."

I leaned in and tried to read the stupidity on her face. "Could you please not turn your daughter into another lost bitch?"

"What is that supposed to mean?"

I turned my attention to the little girl and smiled. "Darling, from the first day you meet a man, you tell him what you think about everything. If he doesn't like it, he wasn't worth it."

Her mother bobbed her head. "Well, yes, that's prudent advice. I was just telling her—"

"You were just telling her how to be a bitch."

"Please, not around the child."

The little girl joined us. "It's okay, Mommy, Daddy says it all the time."

I sat in audience as those two squared off.

"When does your father say that?"

"Well, when I stay with him and Donna, I hear him call you the Bitch of Bendover."

"He what?"

"He calls you—"

"Never mind, I heard you the first time."

I winked, "Aren't exes great."

I should have stopped at that because I had her eating from my lap, but I had to take it across the line, "They peg us so well."

"Typical male thing to say." She returned to her daughter, "Well, your father is no winner, trust me."

As much as I wanted to explain that one parent pitting a child against the other parent amounted to a fucked-up child, I had no skin in the game, hell, I didn't have children. One more teenage prostitute hanging out on First Street wouldn't wreck the world anymore than it already was.

Outside, the five-o'clock viewing of the water fountain's show, spewing to the tune of Dvorak's string quartet #12, spun everyone in joint. As though mummified, all eyes concentrated on the dancing water. I'd become anesthetized. Every hour, from eight a.m. until I went home, that fucking thing went off. Thankfully, they played a different tune each hour or I'd have hanged myself off my window ledge.

I wondered if the water show brought Ms. Hallorin here. Did she sit in this spot and get all moist thinking about how life could have been different if that one man, who could have kept her from becoming a writer, had taken her away and dined her on caviar and champagne?

When the spectacle ended, people cleared out. It dawned on me customers came for the show. With empty tables, my two roommates moved out. I hadn't noticed until the little girl stood, she had a doll in her lap. Ten-years old and she played with a doll—in public. I wondered if she had some sort of fixation issues. I bet she sucked her thumb. Her mother had a shapely build, which made her bitchiness all the more believable. She didn't salute me when they left, but I did get the stink eye. She needed to put that ten dollars away and save up for a bitchlift.

Chapter 6

Across the fountain, I could see the theater marquee, and with it, a new movie coming soon—an erotic thriller. From everything I'd read from my mystery writer, she'd view this film sooner or later. Something else caught my eye. Beside the theater, a new restaurant opened, and inside, a bar. I needed a drink.

On my way out the door, I stopped at a street vendor kiosk and bought a pack of cigarettes. I didn't drink much, and I didn't smoke much, but when I drank I smoked. Something about drinking and smoking went together, sort of like KY and a vibrator.

I sat inside that yuppie bar for three hours drinking whiskey cokes and watching sports on enough screens to give someone epilepsy. I hadn't gone out enough because I didn't realize you can't smoke in bars anymore. Seriously, you can't smoke in bars anymore. Something about health reasons, which considering we're in a place sticking ethanol into our liver, strikes me as fucking retarded. Nonetheless, they forbade me from lighting up, so I sat at a lonely table with a bowl of salty peanuts watching a smorgasbord of sports. Young men talked statistics like Vegas bookies and the women appeared to want to be young men. They debated the virtues of defense over offense as well as any team coordinator. I'm shocked to say that playing a love song so you can get down a girl's pants is gone; those young women might have worn jocks and had hairy nuts. The joint didn't have a jukebox, pool tables, or dartboards, just overwhelming TV screens.

A young woman with less clothing than a lifeguard asked me if I wanted another. She held a tray high like a lantern and gave me an eyeful of tit. I slipped the photo of Dee from my case. "Have you ever seen this woman?"

She smiled. "Comes in here every so often." She brought the tray down and set it between us. "Say, she's not in trouble is she?"

"No, why?"

"Well, you sort of look like a cop."

Half shaven, dressed like a slob, yeah, I suppose I did. "No, just a possible client."

Her eyes lit up as though I might be a tipper. "Are you an attorney?"

"Oh, hell no."

"A private detective?"

"Sorry, wrong again."

She stood with a stupid blank roll-call on her face, as though no one answered 'here.'

"I'm a publisher."

"You make brochures and business cards?"

I shook my head. What a mental midget. "What the...no, that's a printer. I take a thousand rocks and polish them, when I find one that shines, I call it an author. Mostly, I deal with loose gravel that you couldn't make a good street with."

"So you work on roads?"

I put my hands to my face and rubbed tension from my sockets. I had a Mensa on my hands. "Yes, that's it exactly."

"Does that make a lot of money?"

I could tell this conversation had dead ends, so I steered her back on track. "Can you bring me one more, and then close out my tab?"

The sun perched above the rim of buildings circling the promenade; a warm evening breeze snaked in one side and danced with the palms on the way out. The shops bustled with evening traffic and the businesses above had closed for the day. I noticed my lights on, a lone glow of light among the second floor proprietors. "Hmm." I'm not the kind of guy to leave lights on, waste of my gawd-damn money.

I worked my way up the stairs and down the hall. I realized I didn't leave my lights on; rather, someone had broken in.

Son of a bitch.

They fucked up my lock, and the door molding had a chunk out of it. At least they didn't shatter the glass. I'm not sure what the hell they hoped to get from a publisher, I don't deal with cash. Inside, my place looked like an explosion of paper. They'd emptied my filing cabinets, every document, contract, and manuscript strewn across the room. Had to be pretty disappointing for the numbnuts who hoped for a payday. They didn't take anything of importance because anything that might be important, I kept at home. They accomplished pushing me to clean my place. I kept a lot of work I swore one day I'd revisit; but in truth, after seeing my mysterious writer's work, I didn't need to revisit those hacks. I might be able to squeeze a dime out of a few shitty pieces if I expertly marketed their work, and that struck me as too much work. I'd had enough whiskey in me to not give a shit about cleaning up. The maintenance would see the damage and toss a lock on it before morning. I wanted to go home.

Chapter 7

The promenade had one flaw, with refurbished buildings built in an era where everyone parked on the streets, a parking garage stood separated by a dark, lonely alley. People bitched about it, mostly women, and I could see why. For a hundred yards, you were on your own. I had entered that wasteland when I stumbled into four young men; I mean I literally stumbled into them. I have no idea if one of the young gents had just lost his girlfriend, or if he'd taken cock in his ass by mistake, but he acted like one disgruntled human being.

He shoved me. "Do you have a problem, old man?"

Forty-nine wasn't that old, but I guess to a twenty-one year old, it was ancient. "Sorry, just going home."

He continued backing me up until he had me pinned against the alley wall. In the glow of amber lamps, he said, "You aren't going anywhere."

He couldn't have weighed more than a buck fifty, but I don't think he had an ounce of fat. I might have had eight inches and seventy pounds over him, but I wasn't in condition to duke it out, and by the looks of his friends, I was about to fight four of them. "What do you want?"

"I want to kick your ass."

I put my hands up like bumpers to keep us from being dance partners. "I'm not a fighter, I'm a lover."

"You're just a fat piece of shit."

I worked some levity in. "I know, and to think I was once a track star."

He took a step back and eyed me from head to toe. "You, a track star?"

"Yep."

"I bet I could beat you."

I glanced at the end of the alley. "I'll tell you what, I'll race to the end of the alley and back, if you beat me, you can kick the shit out of me."

"How about I just kick the shit out of you instead?"

"Then I guess we'll never know if you can beat me."

He turned to his friends and laughed. "This should be fun." He spun back around. "You're on."

His three friends moved aside. The young man and I lined up, bent over, and took off. The kid had me by ten yards when he made it to the turn; however, if he thought I planned on finishing that race, he had another thought coming, and if he thought I planned to let his stiff penis talk shit to me, he was wrong on that count as well. When he made the turn and came back my direction in a full gallop, my right fist dropped him hard as he passed me. I didn't lose a beat and scurried through to the garage. A hundred yard head start gave me plenty of time to get to my car and bolt out the exit.

Chapter 8

Damn, I wished I'd taken two aspirin before bed. After a repeat performance of draining half my fucking coffee down my shirt, I sat in my office, coming in from the street, afraid my chicken-shit sucker punch might get me killed. My head throbbed, and I hadn't picked up a single sheet of paper. In my swivel comfy chair in the middle of the room, I tilted my head to keep the pounding at a minimum when someone knocked at my door. Christ, I hoped four young men were not at the other end of that knock. "Come in."

"Jeezus, what the hell happened to your door?" Don, a podiatrist across the hall, eyed the frame of my entryway as he pushed his way in.

"They must have mistaken my office for yours." I stared at the ceiling.

"Did Hal come by with a smarmy looking attorney?"

"You mean, Jim, Jim Hunter? Yeah. I take it they hit you up too?" I rolled my head and caught view of Don. He had a stethoscope draped over his shoulder. "Why do you have a stethoscope? You look at feet."

"I think Stella is fucking clients next door. I was trying to listen through the wall."

Stella had a massage business, and attractive left that station years ago—if it ever existed. If she fucked clients, she had pretty desperate clients. "What did you find out?"

"That stethoscopes don't work very well at hearing through walls."

I stood and stepped around paper like a minefield. I came to the door and peeked out at Stella's door. "What makes you suspect Stella is running a brothel?"

Don joined me; our two bodies leaned out into the hallway. "I heard her screaming like a Banshee last night, like she was getting it real good."

"How'd she look when she came in this morning?"

"She didn't come in."

Stella drove a pink Thunderbird, the little coupe. She liked to park on the street, hard to miss, and I didn't miss it that morning. "Her car is here."

Don squinted. "Really? I haven't heard a peep from her."

"Go check on her. Maybe someone fucked her to death." I winked.

We stood there a few minutes shooting the shit when a middle-aged woman walked past us and entered Stella's room. No sooner did the woman enter, we heard a scream of horror.

Don said, "Oh, shit."

That was no 'You scared me' scream. We rolled in behind the woman and Stella's place looked like someone painted her walls in blood, in Stella's blood, because in the center of the reception area the body of Stella, or at least I think it was Stella's body stretched out over the carpet. Hard to tell since it was missing a head. "Fuck me." Those whisky cokes felt like coming up, and I had to swallow a little back down. "Call the cops." I turned to the woman, who hadn't dropped a beat, just one steady stream of high pitched howls. "Shut up!" She reeled it back to a series of short tearful breaths. "Just breathe, honey."

Don pulled out his phone while I put my arm around Stella's client and led her to a chair. "I need you to sit here and not touch anything." She wouldn't take her hands away from her mouth, so I doubted she'd move until the police told her to get her carcass out of there.

Ten minutes later, we heard the sirens, five minutes after that, a fat donut-eating detective with a perky little black chick in a blue uniform arrived. Not the contingent I expected. For Christ sake, it was a dead body; I would have expected half the department to show up.

With a fat detective sporting a hard-on for a gruesome case, I could tell this wouldn't go well.

"I'm Detective Littleton…" and that's all I heard. I went on auto pilot as I thought how his name sounded like a contradiction. 'Little–ton.' Is that possible. Isn't a ton a ton? I faced off with him and pretended to follow along and picked up enough when Don said, "6:45."

He turned to me. "How about you?"

"When I got here, or when I left last night?"

He inched up to me. "Who said anything about last night?"

"Well, considering I wasn't listening to anything you said after you gave that ridiculous name, you're lucky I narrowed it down at all."

"I see we have a smartass in our midst."

"Guilty as charged, provided we're talking about being a smartass and not a murderer."

Don shook like a cold, wet puppy. "I can vouch for him, I got here before him."

The detective crossed his arms like an angry father. "This would go a lot easier if you put the antics aside."

"This would go ten times easier if you let that cute little Angie Dickinson interrogate me."

"Who?"

"Police woman." I always picked up a little jungle fever when ethnic women were around.

He asked, "What's your name?"

"Dillard, Richard Dillard, but you can call me Dick. Everybody does."

"So what time did you get here?"

"Eightish."

"Which offices are yours?"

Don pointed to his, and I motioned to the one across from his. I offered, "I was broken into last night."

That piqued Littleton's interest. He leaned back and called for his assistant.

Flak jacket or not, that was a smokin' hot chick. Couldn't have been taller than five three, callipygous ass, caramel skin, and underneath that jacket had to be a hard C cup. Gravity hadn't fucked up her build, and she didn't strike me as a mom, so those tits hadn't gone all National Geographic on her.

"Take Mr. Dillard over to his office and find out what's been taken."

She stood like a doe, unaware of our conversation.

"I was broken into last night."

Detective Littleton stepped back into Stella's office and the Nubian officer and I headed to mine, leaving Don and Stella's client standing in the hall. I turned and whispered, "Hey, she's got an open hour, see if she needs her feet checked." I rubbed my thumb and fingers together like easy money.

I entered my office with my escort. "Wow, what happened here, Mr. Dillard?"

"Your guess is as good as mine."

"What do you do?"

"I'm a publisher."

"No offense, but I can't imagine you have much to steal in here. Is there anything missing?" She went to my desk and looked without touching. "You have a nice computer."

"They didn't touch it. I don't think they took anything." I stepped further in and came up alongside her. "Officer—"

"Black." She reached to her name plate on her vest and tilted it for me to read.

"Seriously?"

"Seriously what?"

Well, at least hers made more sense than Littleton's. "Nothing." I smiled. "I'm Dick."

She nodded, moved around me and scanned the room. She knelt and used the eraser end of a pencil to shuffle papers. "Are all these manuscripts?"

"Pretty much."

She continued to the door. "Your door has been jimmied, but the massage office wasn't."

"Okay."

"I'd say you were hit first. I doubt they continued after they killed her."

"Maybe they are two separate criminals, two separate crimes."

She nodded. "Maybe, but I'm not a big believer in coincidences. What time did you leave last night?"

"Usual time, but I came back and stayed here until around nine."

"Was your place hit yet?"

"Yeah."

"Why didn't you call the police?"

I waved my hand around the room. "Because they didn't get anything. It's not like they committed murder."

"Have you ever had a massage from your neighbor?"

I didn't know what she meant. Had I ever shagged her? "No, I'm not much of a massage guy. How about you?"

She smiled, "No, I'm not either, but my significant other is."

Damn it, the dreaded other man line.

"She goes all the time."

"I'm sorry, what?"

"My girlfriend goes all the time."

Ah fuck! A dyke.

This cute little thing played for the other team. Not that if she was available, I'd stand a chance, but a man can dream can't he?

Speaking of dreaming…ah forget it.

"Mr. Dillard, you look like you have something on your mind."

"Just thinking about something."

"Is it important?"

I grinned. "No, it's definitely not important."

Chapter 9

Staff from the morgue came to take Stella's body away, and let me be clear, we weren't really sure the body belonged to Stella because without the head, it just looked like her fat carcass, and I couldn't tell one fat middle-aged woman's body from the next, so I went on the pleasant assumption the stiff in her office belonged to someone else.

I busied myself cleaning up after the ebony princess dusted for fingerprints and gave me the go ahead to play house. So nice of the carpet-muncher to give back my space. I felt for Don. I didn't get customers, so the yellow tape across Stella's door didn't mean shit to me, but his business would suffer. However, with the police foot traffic, no pun intended, you would have thought he'd have been wise enough to put up a sign, 'We're Slashing Our Prices, Head On In!' Instead, he holed up in his office and put an 'Out to Lunch' sign on his door.

With all the electricity about the place, I hadn't the time to worry about my mysterious writer, but wondered if she sat in some shop in the promenade watching events unfurl on the second floor. With twenty cop cars downstairs, we'd garnered plenty of attention. I hoped that didn't scare her away.

I'd have felt for Stella and admitted her day had been crappier than mine had a couple not pushed their way through the police line to pay me a visit. Knee deep in pathetic manuscripts, Muffin McCready and her beau checked up on me. Muffin, or as I liked to call her, the former Mrs. Dillard, pranced in with the stench of death.

"Dick!"

I lifted myself from the floor as she blessed me with a gentle waft of Chanel. "They let you through?"

"I told them I was next of kin." She circled me, took off her fur coat, and made Charles, her eunuch husband, hold it like a coat rack.

I glanced at him and shook my head. Sorry bastard. I asked her, "You related to Stella these days?"

"Actually I prayed it would be your door all taped up."

"Great, then it'd look like your door." I motioned to her crotch.

"Fuck you, Dick."

"I believe that's why we're no longer married, Muffin, because you wouldn't fuck me."

She let out a breath and wound up, but Charles, to his credit, backed her down. "Muffin, he's not worth it."

Gay populations exist because of Muffin, she did that to men, and had every woman on the planet been like her, we'd be extinct. "No Muffin, I'm really not worth it." I leaned against a file cabinet and continued, "As much as I'd like to believe you came up here to see that I was okay, I suspect you have business. Get on with it."

"I was checking on my interest."

Thanks to a judicial system with more holes than a breached diaphragm, her attorney had cum all over my face in our divorce.

Somehow, this woman, who'd never worked a fucking day in her life, managed to wrestle twenty-five percent of my company from me. "Well, as you can see, I'm in the middle of my own issues right now." The room still had the odor of break-in.

She blurted, "I'm selling my interest in the company."

I viewed her poker face and explained, "You can't."

"Oh yes I can, as long as I provide you with the opportunity to match the offer."

"Well, I can't think of another human being I'd rather have as a partner less than you, so be my guest."

Know thy enemy, because nothing prepared me for her next sentence.

"I will inform Jim Hunter it's a deal then."

"Whoa there, lily pad, did you just say Jim Hunter?"

"Do you know him?"

"Know is a bit of a strong word. I know he's more of a cunt than you are, and if I'm trading cunts, I'd rather keep the nasty shriveled up one I have now."

Muffin approached and pointed a bony finger. "You know, for someone trying to influence me, you aren't very good at it."

I had to play nice. "What would you like from me?"

"I'd like you to consider moving your office and let Charles set up his C.P.A. practice here."

I heard the words. "I'm sorry, what?"

"I said—"

"I was being rhetorical. Sorry but that's a deal breaker." I knew her, she would sublet it or flat sell the space to Hunter.

She inched in closer, acted like a wife, and touched my cheek. With her pinned-back eyes and Botox lips, she stated, "That's your problem, Dick, you don't know when trouble is staring you in the face."

Her charm didn't faze me—neither did that Freddy Kruger smile. I whispered, "Would you like to feel my penis?"

She volleyed. "Would that please you?"

"Yes, because you'd discover it's as soft as ice cream right now."

"Be that as it may, either you give up this place, or I take up Mr. Hunter on his offer."

"How much?"

"Half a million."

"Holy shit. Jim Hunter has overvalued Dillard Publishing a bit. He's willing to give you a half mil for twenty-five percent of a company that earned under a hundred grand last year?"

"He says there's potential."

There was, but they didn't know that. I had a manuscript from a writer who could change my life; however, splitting it with the likes of either my ex or a little faggot like Hunter wasn't going to happen. "We get residuals on three books, only one of them to any large amount. That's the extent of our success. If it wasn't for, 'Big Butts, Bitches, and other Bedtime Stories,' we'd have shuttered our doors years ago."

Muffin turned and pointed to Charles to hand over her coat. "I don't really care. Either give us this office, or pay a half million dollars for my share of the company," she turned, "or prepare to have Jim Hunter so far up your ass he'll be able to see the polyps on your soul." She smiled. "You have two days to decide."

Chapter 10

Two days. Two days is forty eight hours, and knowing Muffin, all the begging and pleading wouldn't earn me a minute more. God, I hated that bitch. A half million dollars hadn't been at my disposal in like, forever. I'd have sold my house but the courts did that for me when Muffin and I divorced, and she fisted me up the ass.

I scooted papers around the floor like I had Muffin's head in my hand and I taught her a lesson for shitting on the floor, rubbing manuscripts on the wood like sandpaper. "Bad girl!"

"Excuse me?" A girl with an apprehensive knock against my broken door stood there. She couldn't be much more than a teenager.

"Knock like you mean it." I shoved paper into a pile and continued cursing Muffin's name. "How does that feel, huh? You like that, Muffin?"

"Is this Mr. Dillard's office?" I would have pointed out the obvious, since she tapped against the name on the glass, but she beat me to it. "Of course it is, only says so on the door."

"I'm busy, come back another day." To be left alone in times of grief.

She ignored my request and stepped in. "If you don't mind me asking, who are you talking to?"

"Satan's mother."

41

The kid had spunk. "I think I met her. Red hair, puffy lips, walked a step ahead of the man she was with?"

That caught my attention. "One and the same." I asked, "How'd you get in, I know they are prescreening people, and by the looks of your age, unless you're on a ride-along, I doubt you're with the coroner's office."

"They let family through."

I stood, sad for the kid. "I'm sorry. I didn't know you were related to Stella. I apologize for my rudeness."

"I'm not related to Stella."

"What are you some high school newspaper reporter looking for a scoop?" I shook my head. "You got chops, I'll give you that." I motioned for her to come all the way in. My office wasn't long on hospitality. The only chair in the place was mine. I liked to make people stand like they addressed the courts. I took refuge in my comfy chair and watched her squirm.

"No, I'm actually a freshman in college, Mr. Dillard. You are Mr. Dillard aren't you?" She didn't seem too receptive to feeling uncomfortable and plopped her bony ass down onto my desk.

"That I am. Dick Dillard, publisher extraordinaire, but that doesn't tell me much about you, and since you're visiting me, might I ask why it's important enough for you to lie to the police and tell them you are related to a deceased woman just to make my acquaintance?"

She crossed her arms and stared at my door. "I never said I was related to that lady, I said I was related to you."

"And why would you do that?"

Her chin spun to her shoulder faster than Regan MacNeil. With a grin, she offered, "Because I am."

I studied her face, sort of reminded me of my sister when she was that age, gangly brunette who preferred an androgynous look. I put my elbows on my desk and rested my chin on clasped fingers. "Lay it on me." Either my brother, the Jesus freak minister, had stuck his noodle in a congregation member, or I had a child out there I didn't know about. Something told me to lay odds on the latter.

"I'm your daughter." She studied me as hard as I studied her.

"Well of course you are, and how did I come about being your father?"

"You were a panelist at the Oak Valley Writer's Workshop in 1995?"

I jogged my memory, not that I wasn't a panelist there but if I'd slept with a participant of the seminar. How unethical that would have been. "I can't recall sleeping with anyone there."

"According to my mother, you didn't do much sleeping."

The kid had a point. "I still don't recall 'being' with anyone; after all, I was married to Satan's mother at the time."

"Let me jog your memory, my mother said she fell hard for you and slept with you on day one. On day two she caught you in bed with another writer who also fell hard for you."

Now that rang a bell. "Look kid—"

"Are you so self absorbed that you can't even ask my name? Gawd, you're a tool."

This had to be my kid. "What is it?"

"What is what?"

"Your name?"

"Why do you care?"

"Jesus. Look, I'm not going to do this dance with you. You can call me an ass, you can berate me for the shitty life you had never knowing your father, but if you want to settle this, then quit acting ten."

If she'd had a gun, I would have been dead. She slid off the desk, came around the corner and stared down at me with a death grip on my soul. "My name is Richelle; my friends call me Richy, of which you will never be entitled to call me."

"So let me guess, you need money."

Just before a storm approaches, there's eerie electricity in the air. You can smell it, you can feel it. You know a storm is coming, and you need to take shelter.

"What did you just ask?"

"What else could you want?"

"Oh, my God," She backed up and tears raced down her face like tire tracks. "Mom was right, coming here was the stupidest thing I could have done."

"Richelle," I lifted myself from my chair, and every step I took toward her, she took two steps back. When she made it to the door, I stopped to prevent her leaving. "Believe me, if I had known you existed, I would have reached out myself. I never had kids. I always wanted kids, but as you can see, that creature I was married to didn't want to flaw that body. It was the only decent thing she owned."

"I've heard enough, Mr. Dillard. What I've discovered is you were a philandering publisher who used your position to sleep with unsuspecting college students while your wife sat at home suspecting nothing. I will tell my mother who you are and that she should have nothing to do with you."

"Fair enough." I offered, "You have come with some pretense that you can shame me out of who I am." I gathered my senses. "But the reality is, I have to live with myself and I like me. Am I proud of myself over my indiscretions twenty years ago? Not really, but if you knew Muffin, you might understand why I wasn't at home in bed with her. As for you, I have no idea if you had a dad or not, but I hope you grew up balanced. I'd like to think any child of mine did."

"I never had a dad, and I guess I never will." She flung my door wide and left.

I followed her out to the hallway and watched her bang on the elevator button. It slid open and before she closed it, I asked, "What was your mother's name?"

The doors closed as she answered. "Dee Hallorin."

Chapter 11

"Wait!" Too late, the elevator closed.

Shit, damn it.

Figures I'd fuck up and produce a kid with the best writer I'd ever seen and alienate her in the process. I ran for the stairwell only to find out why Richelle used Otis. They'd closed off the stairs for forensics. Evidently, they'd found Stella's head. By the time I'd made back to the elevator and screamed for the bloody thing to come back up it was too late. I wandered around a busy promenade seeking my daughter, but she'd high-tailed it out of there, I'm sure with the intent of telling her mother about the horse's ass she'd met.

I circled the fountain a couple of times and nothing. Well, sort of nothing, on my last pass I bumped into some old friends. Four young men waited for me on my last pass, one with a black eye from hell. "Nice shiner, did your girlfriend give you that?"

They drew closer, and I sighed. One chance and one chance only. "You guys might kick my ass, but I promise you I will track every one of you down. Are you prepared for that?"

Turns out they were, because they wasted no time surrounding me.

"Really, right here in broad daylight, with a dozen cops in and out of that building?" I pointed over to my office.

My main adversary, the one I popped, said, "I'm sure we can find a secluded spot."

I wanted to avoid that scenario. "Very well, lead the way." Yeah, as though I planned on going with them.

Idiots.

They broke formation, and I bolted when they gave me a clear path, punching the kid a second time; this time, sending him backwards into the fountain. Two stayed to get him and the other chased me past 'Forever 21' and the 'Disney Store.' Shit, this started growing old. The fattest one of the bunch followed me, and he might have been thirty years my junior, but I thought about stopping a few times to make sure he wouldn't have a heart attack.

How the hell do kids let themselves go like that? Maybe a little less time on internet porn and a little more time in bed with a porn star might open up those arteries.

"Mr. Dillard! Where are you running off to?" There in front of me, looking as beautiful as any lesbian I'd ever laid eyes on, Officer Black expected me to stop. Behind me, Humpty Dumpty did a turn and headed the other way.

My lungs coughed out, "I saw your beautiful face and ran over here to see if I could carry your gun for you."

She smiled. "Who's your friend?"

I turned and joined her watching him walk away. "A poet. He's discovered I have no use for them."

"A poet?"

"The lowest form of writer." I tried to catch my breath. "Any chance you could give me mouth to mouth?"

"Excuse me?"

"If I have a heart attack?"

"You'll be fine."

It was worth a shot.

"So are you heading up to the second floor?" I stayed close to Black.

She sized me up. "If I didn't know better I'd say you need an escort."

I don't know if you can smell fear, but it radiated from me. "Just thought we could catch up on what you found out about my break-in."

"Well considering that I've had all of two hours to send off the fingerprints, not much." We strolled toward the entry of the building; my four boyfriends now knew in which building I worked. They followed, but I didn't think they'd come in. I figured that would come later.

We passed an officer manning the elevator and entered. As it closed, the four young men stood outside the glass doors of the building. Black winked. "We'll be up there all day, I'm sure you won't have any customers today."

"Well, that's good because I have to clean up my office."

I hit the second floor, and she said, "Besides, who needs poets right?"

"Exactly."

When we made it to my floor and worked our way to my office, Black observed, "Shouldn't the maintenance man fix that?"

"I sort of thought he'd get on it last night."

She asked, "Have you seen him today?"

"Eddy? No, but that's not unusual, he walks through once a day, usually late at night and makes sure the janitors have locked up."

"So doesn't that strike you as odd?"

"A little."

"I'm going to have someone come fix your lock, okay?"

"Is there a problem with Eddy?"

She asked, "Is he smart?"

"Not particularly."

"Well, I would suspect the only problem with Eddy is his health. He has keys to all these offices, so breaking in wouldn't be necessary; however, stumbling across someone breaking in might have left him in the same condition as Stella."

"Unless—"

"It's two separate crimes. I know, but I'm an odds player, Mr. Dillard. Just like if I were playing odds on who wins, you versus the four poets, I'm riding with the poets." She tapped me on the stomach, pointing out my second trimester look, "No offense, but I'm taking them if it's four on one."

"Thanks for the confidence."

"Oh, I'm confident. I'm confident they beat your ass, but don't worry, it won't happen on my watch."

I guessed she saw a more than I thought. "So you're worried a little more for Eddy than about Eddy?"

She continued on down the hall as I stood in front of my door. "Pretty much, Mr. Dillard. Be careful."

Chapter 12

I could have sworn Officer Black said she would keep the riff-raff out of the building, but no sooner than I had set about cleaning my shit up, the door popped open and that dumb fuck attorney stood there like a tramp.

"Looks like you have a mess, Mr. Dillard."

I paid no attention. "Close that door on your way out."

"Listen," his voice slid into conciliation. "I think we got off on the wrong foot the other day."

"Was that my foot up your ass, or yours in your mouth?" I put aside my duties and retreated to my seat. If he wanted to have a discussion, he would stand there like a school boy at the principal's office.

"Can we put aside the hostility and discuss some business?" He came all the way in and danced around my mess.

On his face, I could detect victory, a confidence that he knew he had a stronger hand. "We have no business, Jim, Jim Hunter." I wondered aloud. "How the fuck did you get up here, don't tell me you claimed relations with Stella too?"

"Mr. Dillard, Mr. Dillard, Mr. Dillard, I'm in partnership with Hal, and I wanted to make sure my future office and business was safe."

We understood each other; he was an asshole and determined to prove it. He attempted to sit on the corner of my desk, but I slid my monitor out far enough to take up the space. He took the hint and retreated to his favorite spot, peering out my slatted blinds.

"You see anything out there that makes your Willy swell?"

He maintained his gaze out my window. "You're about as pleasant as a cockroach."

"You'd know all about cockroaches, I suspect."

He turned. "Do you know Muffin McCready?"

I hate rhetorical questions unless I'm the one asking them. "Too bad she's married, you two would make an awesome couple."

He held his arms out like he wanted to hug me. "And to think she's either going to bring us together as partners, or hand this office over to me."

I rested against my chair; let the leather embrace me as I watched him work his pitch. "You getting this office isn't going to happen."

"Really? Mr. Dillard, you have five hundred thousand dollars floating around somewhere?"

I acknowledged. "I don't, but I don't suspect when push comes to shove, your daddy will let you take the car out for a spin. Something tells me you're about as responsible as a whore in a dildo shop."

Jim stepped forward and leaned over my desk. I'd crawled beneath his skin because his tan had a red hue to it. "I will have you for my own personal lunch, you dick wad."

"You might want to reconsider that. Some would say I'm a pretty tough piece of leather. You could be chewing for days before you realize I'm choking the shit out of you."

Jim straightened and laughed, sort of like a little girl who doesn't want to admit the jokes on her. "You are a piece of work. Any other venue and I'd want you by my side, but make no mistake—I'll crucify you on this deal."

"Are you sure you want to be a partner in my business, Mr. Hunter?" I stood so we reflected a difference in height. I cast a shadow over him. "Because if this goes through, who do you think is going to be the pitcher and who will be the catcher? Trust me, after my dick is so far up your ass, don't expect a reach around. All I will want to hear from you is a steady stream of crying, because you will be my bitch.

"I'm telling my dad what you said."

Did he just threaten me with running home and telling on me?

"You see that door over there?" I shoved my index in the direction to the exit. "I want you to find it. I want you to find it without so much as a peep out of your pie hole."

He positioned himself to respond.

"Ah, ah, ah, I mean it, keep it shut."

He hiked up his slacks. I suspected his dick, which he clearly used to hold them up when he entered, had deflated and he had no support. He turned and made a beeline for my pile of papers.

"And if you kick that pile, I can promise you, I will bounce your head against the floor so hard you'll see yesterday's bowel movement."

He hesitated as he reached the pile. His foot wound up but I suspected his nuts had sucked so far up into his stomach that he released a little dribble onto his skivvies. He hopped over and made it to the door. Unwilling to let me defeat him, he took a shot. "Mark my words, you will hear from my dad."

Chapter 13

I needed to do something fast. Two days would come and go before I knew it, and I had no plan. Even though my ex deserved zero rights to breathe oxygen, a waste of humanity, wishing she could join Stella had bad karma written all over it. I could destroy an entire day fantasizing about kicking her head into a goal.

Don peeped out of his hole like a groundhog. "You want to do lunch?"

"Do lunch? You've been hanging out in the valley too much." I waved him in.

"Come on, let's get out of here."

"Business slow, huh?"

He shrugged. "They aren't letting anyone up."

How I wished that was true. They've let every pain in my ass up so far.

"Yeah, let's go eat."

"Have you tried that sports bar yet?"

"The one with the jiggling titties? Yeah, I'm game to go back." I noticed Don had an otoscope in his breast pocket. "What the hell do you have an ear doctor's magnifying tool in your pocket for? You're a foot doctor."

"There's been this pinhole gap between our two offices for years; I wanted to see if I could see anything in Stella's office."

"Did you discover anything?"

"That otoscopes don't work very well for spying."

I joined Don in the center of my room. "You need to stop that."

"Stop what?"

"Spying."

"Why?"

I coaxed him out into the hallway, and nodded to a police officer. "I'm going out, can you make sure that no one drops off anymore trash to my place?"

"Worry about your own stuff."

I love that they are here to serve and protect. At what point do my tax dollars pay for them to harass and be pricks?

"Okay then, enjoy your sack lunch your wife made for you."

"Do you always have to be rude to people?" Don found authority overwhelming, and from his submissiveness, I gathered he preferred I not draw attention from them.

"Honestly, I don't really care. I read shit manuscripts every day, and am filled with a cache of things writers should have said but didn't. Because I don't get a chance to express it on paper, other than in my quippy rejection letters, it has to come out somewhere, Don."

"You know I have a book in me."

Oh Jesus, Lord above, and for the love of God, do not let this man tell me about a book he believes he is destined to write.' But I know better.

"What's it about?"

"It's about interstellar travel through worm holes."

I employed my three response method as I tuned him out. 'Uh huh,' 'I see,' 'Okay.'

We made it to the elevator. Don kept yapping. I said, "Uh huh."

At the ground floor, I scanned the area outside the glass doors, "I see."

We hurried around the fountain and across the promenade. "Okay."

We made it without being detected by my four alley fans. "So what do you think?"

"About what?"

"My story."

"Sounds like a winner."

I don't know why I encourage people.

"Really? You really think I should go for it?"

Does that mean he'll be bothering me constantly? Or will he peter out by page two, rewriting those same ten sentences every five hours, determined to perfect them ad nauseam?

"A man has to create his opus some day, Don. If you haven't found it in all those feet you try to get nasty rashes off of, then why not write a story about space travel."

"Will you help me?"

Ah, shit.

"I'll tell you what, you have a half million dollars I can borrow for a little while, I'll consider it."

"If I did, how long before you paid it back?"

"How old are you now?"

"Forty three."

"What's the age of retirement?"

Don stopped me. "I don't have it, and that's too long."

"Just as well, I doubt I would have paid you back anyway."

"So why the need for money?"

I exchanged glances between Don and a five foot girl with floatation devices. "I'll take dessert, please."

She swept her hand out to the booths. "We have menus for that."

"I bet you do."

She seated us next to a view of the promenade; I found it interesting to see it from the other side. The noon hour had struck and Mozart's Eine Kleine Nachtmusik filled every hollow crack in the yard. Water danced to the rhythm like ballerinas in heat. As usual, the visitors lined up like zombies.

"So you are only getting dessert?"

I watched our waitress wiggle her ass as she moved down the row. "Are you blind?"

"What?" He followed my view. "Oh. Funny. Yeah, she's cute."

"Yeah, something like that."

Don returned to our conversation. "So, why the need for cash?"

I explained my situation and he suggested, "Why not ask for Charles to share your office?"

Charles, as in Muffin's husband?

I had no words. I had no expression.

"Okay, so bad idea, but what other options do you have?"

I didn't know if I did have options, but I had to find my love child's mother and find out if the rest of her book had hope, and then I had to convince her to allow me to publish it. "Slim and none Don, slim and none."

Chapter 14

Don went back to his office, and I dropped by the coffee shop and my favorite barista. "Hey kid?"

"Do I know you?"

"Yeah, I've sat in here the last two days in the spot that woman writer sat in."

"Oh yeah, the one who told me about you."

Well, she didn't tell you about me. If she had, I'm sure you wouldn't be so sweet to me.

"Yeah, that one. Anyway, she drop by at all?"

"I told you she said she wouldn't be coming in for awhile."

"I need to find her. Any chance you know more than you're telling me?"

"As much as I'd like to soak a few more dollars from you, I don't know any more than you do."

"Fair enough." I asked for another one of Dee's drinks and scooted over to our favorite table. Desperate times called for desperate measures. If she was eyeing this spot maybe a sign would help. A little kid beside me drew outside the lines like a spastic, using a green crayon on an elephant in his coloring book. His mother showered him with praise, letting him believe he was the next Rembrandt. "Excuse me, but really?" I shook my head.

"Really what?"

"Shouldn't you be instructing him to stay inside the lines and use the right colors? You think that's good parenting?"

"Why I never—"

"Stop right there, I know you have never. That's apparent." I turned to the kid. "I'll buy one from you if you do me a favor."

He stopped and gave me his attention. "What do you want me to do?"

I reached down and pulled the green crayon from his stubby fingers and tore the sheet from the book. The next page had a Giraffe. "I will pay you five dollars to ask your mother what the color of this animal is, draw it by staying inside these lines, and do the best you can." I pointed out the thick outer tracing lines. "And use the correct colors. Deal?"

His face lit up, and he asked his mother, "Can I?"

She narrowed her contempt for me but acquiesced. "fine."

While Corky from 'Life Goes On,' gave it a real try, I kept the elephant and turned it over to the blank side. I used the green crayon and wrote "Let's talk" across the entirety of the page, big enough to be seen from a good set of binoculars. I retrieved a spot of tape and posted it above my head. I had nothing to lose.

The kid finished, and he drew inside the lines. I said to his mother, "See, a little instruction goes a long way." However, she must not have made it to the zoo in her life, because giraffes aren't orange. Oh well, orange was close enough. I handed the kid a fin, and he handed me his first commissioned piece. I suspected my thirty-second lesson would stick with him a lot longer than his mother's "Here, entertain yourself while I text on my cell phone" instructions ever would.

He held up the bill. "You want me to do another one for you? I'll only charge you four for it?"

Geez, what was this kid's name, Goldberg? "No, that's all right, but I'll cherish this one."

Speaking of Goldberg, I needed to contact my buddy, Abraham, over at Warner. Not much of a phone lover, I still did business on a flip phone, circa Star Trek days. I flipped it open and punched in Abe's number.

"Dick! How's it hanging?"

"Like meatloaf, and you?"

"Not bad. Say, news said they found a headless body over there in one of the buildings in the promenade. Anywhere near you?"

"Yeah, pretty close."

"Anyone you knew?"

Too much small talk.

Every time I spoke to Abe, we bullshitted about nothing. No wonder I never called him. "Hey, I have a favor to ask."

"Shoot."

"I've known you a long time, and I've only brought one piece of work I thought had movie potential, and you took it, and it did."

"You got another one."

I fudged. "I do, and it's the best thing I've ever come across." I reiterated, "Ever."

"Send it on over."

"If you like it, I may need a loan asap."

"Asap as in immediately?"

"Yeah."

"Like ten large?"

"More like five hundred large."

"You're out of your fucking mind."

"Abe, I will shop this around to every studio in the Hollywood. It's that good. I will let you have it. I just need to come up with cash. I'll discount it on the backend and give you a great deal."

"Dick, you are out of your mind if you think anyone is going to give you a half million dollars to look at a manuscript. Is it in script form?"

"No."

"So you have a novel manuscript that you want a studio to trust from a publisher who has one piece of work converted in his twenty years of business? I want you to put yourself in my position. What high grade designer drugs would I have to be snorting to get you to make that deal?"

"Will you at least take a look at it before you say anything?"

"Of course I'll take a look at it, and if it's as good as you say it is, I'll push the studio to not only script it, I'll have them market the novel for you, but we are talking months and months from now."

I didn't have months; I had two days. What's more, I had two days to keep that slimy attorney from owning twenty five percent of everything. I knew Muffin well enough to know she didn't give a shit about that office; she would turn Faust in a moment for that kind of cash. "Okay."

I gathered my artwork and took down my signage. I could tape them to my office window.

Chapter 15

I taped the giraffe and the 'Let's Talk' facing out my window. Not sure if anyone could see the sign, but perhaps Dee had an eye on my office and paid close attention to my movement. I dialed 411 and asked the voice robot for Dee Hallorin. Back at me came, "Dog houses, is that correct?" I said, "No."

Who has the name Dog Houses? Dumb shit voice recognition.

"Okay, let's try that again, just the city and name of business."

Again, I repeated the city and said, "Dee Hallorin."

"Deep Hallows, is that correct?"

"No!"

Gawd damnit.

A third time it asked me for the city and name, and a third time I said, "Dee," only I drew it out, and then I enunciated fucking clearly, "Hallorin."

"Dean…"

I cut it off with a stream of expletives, followed by, "Operator, operator, operator,"

"One moment, please."

When a human voice came on, she said, "Dee Hallorin, correct?"

65

Now, of course that's correct, but the bigger question was, if they taped my request, then I can assume they taped the rest of my dialogue as well. Amazing how calm she remained, especially after I berated the activated voice's lady parts. Anyone else might have scolded me for my five star bitch-a-thon.

"I'm sorry, but there is no listing with that name."

"Anything in the neighboring cities?"

She answered, "There isn't anything in the state."

"How about Richelle Hallorin?"

"No, sir."

Fuck me.

"Thanks anyway." I had to find this woman. She might tell me to go to hell, she might gloat over having something I needed, with no intention of letting me have it, but I had to know for sure. What did I know? Her name was Dee. What it stood for could be anything, including Dee. Her kid's name was Richelle, and she was a freshman in college. What college? Not a clue. Dee said she lived locally, but in what part of local did that mean. This county had fifteen million people.

I lived in a city with hundreds of high schools, so I couldn't call admissions at every high school and locate my long lost daughter's alma mater. I turned to the computer and typed in Hallorin. Nothing came up. 'Come on, any kid of mine had to have done something notorious enough to turn up on social media.

Nothing.

My door creaked and slid open. Officer Black and a man with a utility belt, looking every bit the part of the Village People, played with my door knob.

"Mr. Dillard, we're going to fix your door for you."

"Yes, I think you told me that already."

She stepped in. "You sound stressed."

Since when did the police work as psychiatrists? Chances were I was a suspect, so looking stressed must have signaled guilt. "I can't find someone."

She stepped closer. "Who?"

This smacked of interrogation. "The mother of my daughter."

"I didn't think you had any children."

It was definitely an interrogation, I never told her anything about my family, if she knew Muffin and I never had children, she'd been snooping. "I didn't think I had any children either."

"What's the name?"

"Why?" Not that I didn't appreciate the interest, but having a cop start prying into my personal life annoyed me.

"Because I might be able to help you." She stood with her hands behind her back at attention.

"Don't do that."

"What?"

"Stand like that."

"Like what?"

"Like a cop."

She swung her arms forward and crossed them against her chest. "But I am a cop."

"Be that as it may, you are too pretty to stand like one."

I'd irritated her. "That's a rather sexist remark."

I held my hands out and swept them around the room. "So, this is my office, and if I want you to look lady-like, that's my prerogative."

"No, that isn't your prerogative. You don't have the right to make sexist remarks, Mr. Dillard." '

"Even if I think you're cute?"

She pointed at me and did her best bad-cop impersonation. "I should taser you right now."

"With or without my clothes on?"

She shook her head. "Wow, you are a piece of work. You are fifty shades of not right. No wonder you are divorced, Mr. Dillard."

"So what about that help?"

She turned back to the repairman, who'd finished up with my knob and jamb. "Forget it, Mr. Dillard, you are on your own."

I think she likes me.

Don poked his head in the door. "You wanted to talk?"

I had my thoughts wrapped around finding my mysterious writer, the vessel of my only child. "What?"

"Your note."

"My note? What the hell are you talking about?"

Don pointed to my window. "Isn't there a note behind those slats that says, "Let's talk?"

What a self absorbed twit.

"And why would I put a note in the window for you?"

He motioned in Stella's direction. "I thought maybe you didn't want the police to know we were talking."

"Why would I care?"

He hesitated, his gaze somewhere only foot doctors go. "Just asking."

"For your information, the note is for a writer I came across this week with a script that might be worth a lot, and don't tell anyone, okay?"

"Why? That sounds like great news." He scanned side to side. "Why don't you have a chair or a couch, or something for people to sit on?"

"Because I don't want people getting comfortable here, and as for the great news, it is great news. Good enough news to make an ambulance chaser want to be my partner. So don't say shit."

He leaned against the wall—too comfortable for me. "Yeah, I get your point."

"Check out my new door. See if it closes properly on the way out." I went back to my computer screen, bringing up variations of Dee's name.

"You're kicking me out?" Don pulled away from the wall, wounded by my rebuke.

"Nothing personal, but you know how I like to be alone."

"I have no patients today, I sort of thought we could hang out."

I waved him off with the back side of my hand. "No, I'm pretty happy talking to the one person who doesn't irritate me."

Don surveyed the room. "But you're the only one here."

"That's right. And I'm not exactly the only one here, you're still here."

He shook his head. "Fine, but if you want to talk, you know where to find me."

"Yes, with your ears and eyes glued to the north side of your office, spying on forensics." As he turned to leave, I noticed a contraption strapped to his belt. "Wait."

Don turned. "What?"

"Open up your jacket."

"This?" He pulled a sigmoidoscope from a holster.

"Why do you have a colonoscopy camera? You're a foot doctor."

He had this shit-eating grin as though he'd given birth to twins. "I finally figured out how to see in that room. I shoved this into the bowels of that crack."

I couldn't believe it. "And what did you learn?"

"Not much, just a bunch of people testing for fingerprints."

"You need to stop that. Pretty soon, they are going to catch you and suspect you are behind her death."

He dismissed my warning and left to do whatever nosy shit he had decided on.

Given my short amount of time left, I had to come up with a better plan than searching the internet and a green crayon sign out the window. Someone tapped on my door. "Go away, Don." They tapped again. "I don't want any company."

I heard a male voice. "It's not Don."

Who now? Please let it not be that little bastard Jim, Jim Hunter and his father. "Come in."

Detective Littleton waddled in. "You have information you want to share with me?"

"About what?" I really wish cops wouldn't be so cryptic. If he planned on accusing me of something, please get on with it.

"You tell me."

I crossed my arms and leaned back in my comfy chair while he shifted from one rotund stub to the other. "Get on with it, detective, I don't have all fucking day to play twenty questions."

"Who is Giraffe?" He stepped closer and examined me. "Is that code for someone?"

"What on god's green earth are you talking about?"

He slapped my desk, the echo jarring any silence awake. "Interesting you say green. You're slipping."

"Excuse me? Have you been abusing the narcotics in the evidence room?"

"Look, Dillard. You have a giraffe, which I assume means something, along with a green 'let's talk' sign in your window. I'm guessing the giraffe is either someone, or somewhere."

This is why I have no faith in the police.

"Giraffe stands for city sewer treatment center, room one, the feces first stage breakdown. Let's talk is to Stella's killer. We're supposed to meet there this afternoon."

Littleton stared me down. "I don't believe you."

"As well you shouldn't. As much as I'd like to tell you to go hang out in a shit factory, the picture, a little kid drew for me, and the note is to a personal acquaintance. The two are not related." I tipped my head in disappointment, "Now, if you don't mind, I'm sort of busy."

"I'm starting to really dislike you, Dillard."

I nodded. "And that's good, because then we'd feel the exact same way about each other." Again I swept a hand gesture to an unwanted guest. "If you please."

Don't they have a fitness test for policemen?

Watching him walk away reminded me of a cow in a downhill race. "Can you grab my out-to-lunch sign on that hook and hang it on the door for me."

"Do it yourself, Dillard." He rattled the glass as he slammed my door shut.

Fucker, better not break it.

Chapter 17

My office phone rang. I'd hoped to hear a sultry voice from an author I desperately needed to talk to, but instead I heard the incessant drone of Mrs. Howard. She had a bit of news for me.

"Mr. Dillard, I just thought I should let you know that a friend of my sister showed my work to a friend of a friend of hers, and that woman thinks my work is outstanding, and she is a major publisher for Random House, as well as a professional editor." She continued at warp speed about how this would be the next 'Fifty Shades of Gray,' of which I had no doubt was already written as well.

I wrestled a 'but' into the conversation, and during her pause to take a breath, I slid in with, "it's still not written very well, Mrs. Howard."

"So says you! And who the hell are you? I have a professional publisher, a real professional publisher telling me otherwise." Her pride whistled through the receiver.

As much as I wanted to wish her luck, I couldn't. This had train wreck written all over it. "So is the publisher Random House?"

"The publisher is an affiliate of Random House."

"An affiliate. You mean like Crown or Doubleday?" Could I have missed something in her work that they didn't?

"Two Princes."

I tapped the keys of my computer with the deftness and speed of a cheetah. "Two Princes, you say?" Since I was a subsidiary, I had the list of all the others. "Princes, as in the royalty title, right?"

"Exactly."

Nothing.

Another self-publisher with grand hopes and zero credibility. "Well, I see you have proven me wrong, Mrs. Howard. I wish you the very best, and I'm sure a worldwide speaking engagement, Oprah, and Inside the Actors Studio are in your future."

"Let this be a lesson to you, Mr. Dillard…" I hung up. I didn't need that woman to discover what 'rude awakening' meant if she lectured me. Of course, she would pay for her own ISBN, barcode, and advertising. There would be no marketing, and the artwork would be from someone's five-year-old son. Good for her.

Let the real lessons be to all the writers out there who think writing is easy and no one needs an editor.

How much farther into shitty could my day fall? I had an ex-wife who wanted to sell her twenty-five percent of my company, an attorney with a hard-on for my really cool office, a kid wanting to fight me, a neighbor with a head rolling around the stairwell, and a writer—who apparently I fathered a child with—out there somewhere with the best damn first three chapters of a book I'd ever laid eyes on.

Two hefty manila envelopes plopped through my door slot, and the tapping of the mailman's shoes echoed from the hallway. I still had a pile of shit in the middle of the room, but why not add to it with two more crappy manuscripts.

I made my way over the debris and caught sight of 'Hallorin' on the top envelope. I grabbed both pieces of mail, opened the other and read the first line. I removed the three chapters and tossed it on the pile. Ms. Hallorin's I carried back to my seat. Inside, she enticed me with another three chapters. What the hell was this woman doing? This was straight up brilliant work.

She wove a tale of a woman dealing with the perils of life, of everyday living that wasn't so every day and not so living. Sprinkling in prose as well as Fitzgerald and telling a tale that would make Bronte jealous, she wrote visceral to its core—the flesh peeled to the bone, and the nerves pulsed with exposure.

I didn't have the option of putting it down; it held me prisoner with every uncovered truth of another human being's soul. She didn't waste her images with throwaways, they went somewhere; her narrative laid the foundation for a journey the point-of-view character traveled, and yet they didn't overshadow her dialogue. Her scenes tightened to a clenched fist with the value of every word mapped out in gold.

Originality oozed from her manuscript. It had transcendent qualities a generation of writers would one day mimic. Power drove the story, but innocence fueled it.

What muses her?

Why had she written this story?

Chapter Six gave me my answer.

Dee Hallorin has written about us.

Chapter 18

Nothing in life is guaranteed.

I should have worked for someone else years ago, but I discovered I didn't fare too well working for others.

I'd had this gig for twenty years, developed a good reputation of publishing well-written material, not always the popular shit, but well written. I'd earned a couple of dimes along the way, and my foul-mood allowance made this job perfect. I'd lost my first two jobs out of college; one for disagreeing with a co-worker, the other for insubordination, both for using the words 'fuck you' while describing the particular feeling I had for them. My third job I lost for sleeping with the boss' wife, and that's a termination you don't ever want to see coming down the hallway. Mr. Jones, a fat little man, and thank God for that, had the desire to beat the living shit out of me. At the time, I thought he deserved having someone sleep with his wife. He was grossly overweight and ten years his wife's senior. He had no business being with the kinky Mrs. Jones, who I might add, taught me several different uses for a cucumber, one of which I hoped to never revisit. Years later, I realized she'd whored herself out and ratted on me because she wanted a new car. If I could go back and apologize to Mr. Jones I would; however, he passed on from a massive heart attack fucking his secretary.

Good for him, paybacks are a bitch, Mrs. Jones.

I always had a predilection for the English language. My mother was a drunken bitch with a silver tongue. She could weave a rant using words a poet would orgasm over. I marveled when the day came to a close, and she'd hole herself up in the house, bottles of gin and vermouth in hand, ready to lay a spew of hate down for anyone within earshot. She'd often ramble in an eloquent tirade against something moronic on television. She didn't discriminate: sports, politics, entertainment, the weather. Poor Dad, he often took the brunt of it, his face buried in his newspaper, answering "Yes, dear" as she reminded him she should have married an attorney, at least then the paperwork would have been at her disposal. He never raised a hand or said a cross word, just went about his business.

However, when Dad passed away, I discovered that next of kin became her point of reference, and I was next of kin. She wondered why I quit coming to visit. She never looked herself in the mirror and took inventory of her own life and the mess she created. She passed away in her garden, telling a gopher to go to hell. The next door neighbors found her holding a trowel, half stuck in a gopher hole and her martini glass still full. Mother had to be dead; she would never have wasted a martini.

I had come to realize my run might be over. That twenty-five percent my ex owned had put me in the poor house. I couldn't live in this city with what leftovers remained. I collected my six chapters of Ms. Hallorin and tossed the rest of the work onto the floor with the pile of other shit manuscripts. I transferred the office phone to my cell and decided to spend the rest of the afternoon away from the CSI across the hall.

I took refuge in Ms. Hallorin's seat in the coffee shop and pulled out my laptop. I hadn't written for my own pleasure in years, given up on the time necessary to write. However, the questions Ms. Hallorin posed and the direction she went called on me to answer. For the next three hours, I tapped away a response; a purging of my soul to a woman who bore a child from an encounter with me.

The sun worked its way down, and I needed to get home. When Muffin left me, she left behind a Siamese kitten, Jinx, and now Jinx lived out her twilight years and didn't like to be left alone in the dark. I stopped by the counter, and I swear that kid never left the shop. "What's good on your little menu?"

"We have a cordon bleu chicken panini to die for."

I winced. "I don't know."

"Just try it." He reached in the display case and pulled out a sample. "Try this." He handed me a small morsel.

"Damn, that's excellent. You sold me."

He took my money and returned with a wrapped sandwich. "You will be buying these every time you come in, mark my words."

I asked. "Do you ever have time off?"

He shrugged. "What for? I don't have a life. I work at a dumb-fuck coffee shop for next to minimum." He leaned over the counter. "What I wouldn't give to have my own business, be established, work my own hours." He nodded, "Sort of like you."

"You'd trade me?"

"In a heartbeat."

"Careful what you ask for."

"Why?"

I scooted closer and lowered my voice. "Because that's a trade I'd make, and I'd be the winner."

"So says you, you don't know what I go through every day."

"Son, I'd give my left nut to be twenty-something again, to fuck all night and still be able to fuck in the morning. To know that a pain shooting across my chest is nothing more than acid reflux from a night of drinking too many whiskeys, but more importantly, to know I'm not looking at the downhill slope to life." I straightened, "But the real tragedy about our two wishes is mine is not possible. I can't go back, I can't regain a youth I miss. You can have your dream; you don't need to trade with me. Think about that." I raised my sandwich in salute and took leave.

Outside, the fountain danced, and Rossini's William Tell Overture told a story. I passed a crowd oblivious to anything but the trance of music. I approached the alley with caution. I didn't need to test my luck against four young men. Sooner or later, they wouldn't be so stupid to buy into anything I said. From one end to the other, a desolate cavern of trash and garbage bins.

As I cleared the first garbage bin, movement startled me and my heart picked up a beat.

"Sorry, didn't mean to scare you." A bum in raggedy clothing, a stench of grime, worthless in every aspect of human endeavor, waved a hand up in friendship.

"It's okay. How are you this evening?"

"I'm fine." His voice beaten down into gravel. "I was teased a little tonight, but sort of comes with the territory."

The odor from the bin overpowered any sense of decency. "What's your name?"

"Why?" My newest neighbor on the block eyed me like I planned to report him.

"Just don't like calling friends, 'stranger.'"

"My name's Tom."

"Tom, I'm Dick."

He chuckled, "Dick, good name."

I smiled, "I like it." I motioned to the trash bin. "This doesn't strike me as a very pleasant spot to pick to bed down."

He rapped the side of the canister. It gonged. "Food!"

The other side of the brick wall housed a P.F. Changs. "Partial to Chinese food, are you?"

"Partial to any food."

I stepped closer. "Tom, here, have this." I handed over my sandwich. "It's still warm, and it's a good change up from all that MSG you must be ingesting."

"MS what?"

"Nothing." I pulled away and headed to the garage.

"Hey, Dick?"

I turned. "Yes."

"Weren't you out here last night? Didn't you drop some young feller who was hasslin' ya?"

"Ah, you were here?"

"I was, right here in this spot."

"Yes, well, hopefully they decided to take a night off."

"Nope. Those were the boys who were teasing me." He held up his fingers. "I picked up a quarter and it was red hot. The apparently heated it up and tossed it to me. When I picked it up, it burnt me, and they had a good chuckle at my expense."

I went back over to Tom and pulled out my lighter. Between us, in the glow of my flame, he held up a blistered thumb. "Why those little pricks. How long ago did this happen?"

"Not too long ago. They said they were going to wait for someone in the garage."

"That would be me." I retrieved a ten from my wallet. "Here, go buy something to drink."

"Anything I want?"

"You've got no caveat on this bill." I gave him the money and tried to shake his hand.

"You don't want to shake my hand. You don't know where it's been." He winked.

I went back out the way I came and entered from the patron entrance. I snuck around the corner and noticed the four young men loitering around the resident stairwell. The stairwell only opened from the inside, the outside remained locked, a safety corridor for tenants of the building. Right next to the door stood the unfortunate young man I'd tangled with. He resembled a raccoon, both eyes darkened from a serious beat down. The other three enjoyed a smoke in the open breezeway. I could hear the little weasel telling his friends that my ass was going to feel his pain. I backed up and took the flight of patron stairs to the second floor. I hurried to the resident stairs and unlocked the door. I dropped down a floor and without hesitating, pushed the door open, and reached around to collar the kid. In one motion, I pulled him inside the resident stairwell and closed the door. Before anyone knew what had happened, I had bounced the kid's face off the steel railing and blood shot from his nose like the fountain in the promenade; he sang like a canary in heat.

I bent over and grabbed the kid by the nape of the neck. "You ever play a prank on a bum again, I swear I will burn half your body, do you fucking understand me?" I don't think he listened to a word I said because, between his yelping and the pounding on the door by his friends, my voice was side noise.

I ran up the steps, out the second floor, past the empty guard station.

They are never there when you need them.

I made it down to the street and figured I'd take the bus. Screw the car. There to my right, I realized I could have avoided all that hassle. I had parked in the street!

Son of a bitch.

Amazing how routine trumps short term memory. I jumped in my car and headed home to give Jinx some company.

Chapter 19

I pulled into my driveway, the condo parking lot, which meant an apartment to me since I rented. At least it had the security of a wrought iron gate. I didn't have the sandwich, and I didn't feel like cooking, so I knocked on Mrs. Oliver's door. She always treated me like her son, and in return I gave the old bird company whenever she felt lonely. She insisted I come over and clear out her refrigerator as often as I needed. That night, I needed.

"Come in, Richard." Her vein riddled hand shook as she fiddled with the screen.

"Let me help you, Mrs. Oliver." I tugged and it unsnapped.

A musty senior odor billowed out into the night air. "Any chance I can pick up a bite to eat?" I pulled out my wallet, and she slapped my wrist.

"Don't be silly. Of course you can. I just happened to have something I planned on sending over to you." I measured my steps so I didn't pass her. "It's there on the counter." She had a sandwich half wrapped in a paper towel.

"What kind of sandwich is that?"

"It's called cordon bleu." She rested her hand on the crux of my elbow and joined me in the kitchen.

I chuckled. "So as you giveth, shall you receive."

"Excuse me?"

I mentioned my encounter with Tom.

"For the measure you use will be the measure you receive, Richard."

Mrs. Oliver liked to recite scripture. "I'm guessing that's in the bible somewhere?"

"That it is, Richard." She oomphed into a stool, surprising me with her power to pull herself up. "It is from Luke, 6:38."

I could feel a sermon coming on, and I needed to get the hell out of there. A sermon, I did not need. No need to save my soul, I had a comfortable spot ready for me right next to the fireplace. "Oh, look at the time, Mrs. Oliver. Poor Jinx is probably yowling for me."

"Oh, Richard, you just got here." Her disappointment crushed me, but I couldn't sit around and listen to Jesus talk. "I'll be back, I promise. Give me a chance to settle in and eat, scratch Jinx behind the ear, and maybe shower. It's been a long day, and I have a lot of interesting news."

She smiled. "Well, I'll be here. Lord only knows for how long, but as long as I am, I'll be here in this place."

I thanked her for the sandwich, a little peck on the cheek, and I high-tailed it to my place. When I unlocked my door, Jinx must have grown tired waiting and taken a spot up on the balcony, her second favorite spot after 'in my ear' on my pillow, suckling on my lobe. After all these years, she still wet my ear every damn night. "Here, Girl!"

Nothing.

I dropped my bag at the door, carried the sandwich into the kitchen and called Jinx one more time. I opened the refrigerator and pulled some cream out. Pouring it into her dish worked every time. She could hear that swoosh from two rooms and one floor away. I waited a minute and realized she must be very busy to not come see Dad.

Her perch, a series of carpeted stairs, tunnels, and ladders overpowered the top floor balcony outside my bedroom, and she would sit out there from the time I left until I came home, waiting patiently for a stupid bird to alight upon the balcony to become her prey. I never witnessed a catch, but be damned if once a month, she didn't have feathers strewn from one end of the bedroom to the other, carcass somewhere in the bowels of her belly.

I flipped on the light, half expecting to find the mutilations of a raptor, but nothing. I went to the balcony, and there in the corner, curled up in a ball, Jinx enjoyed a good nap. I opened the sliding glass door and called her, but she didn't move. I don't know if I realized something didn't feel right, or if I experienced denial, but I called her one more time knowing she wouldn't move. I flipped on the balcony light, stepped to her daybed and knelt down. "Pretty girl, you okay?" I stroked her head, her tongue slightly protruded, her body chilling, her vitals gone. "No, not Jinx." A line of moisture filled the rim of my bottom lids. I picked her up. She still had some give and her body crumpled in my arms. I nestled my face into her neck, the scent of Jinx still fresh. "Sorry, I wasn't here for you, girl."

I slid Jinx's collar off and placed it on my dresser. I pulled my pillow, our pillow, off the bed and placed her comfortably in the depressed pocket. I carried her downstairs and set her and the pillow on the couch while I changed into some jeans and a tee shirt. I went to the basement and grabbed a shovel and a large boot box.

Outside, each unit had a flower garden below the front window. Mine didn't have any flowers. Being the only single man in the complex, my place stood out as a testimony to bachelor living. Maybe that year I'd plant something. Spring was around the corner and even Mrs. Oliver, at her age, continued to plant flowers in her bed. I dug a hole, deep, wide, and with my soul pulling on my heart. When I turned to put Jinx in the box, I couldn't help but notice how comfortable she looked on our pillow. I opened the box and placed her down in, cramped, tight, twisted in a 'We'll make it fit' arrangement. I dug the hole deeper and wider. I went inside and found the box my space heater came in. I carried it out to the yard and put the pillow inside. I removed Jinx and put her back onto the pillow. She looked golden, at peace, on the pillow I shared with her for all these years. I lowered the box into the hole and carefully covered it with dirt. When I finished, I sort of wished Mrs. Oliver could have been there to give one of her bible phrases. She wasn't, so I shrugged. "Ashes to ashes, dust to dust." I took a long, hot shower and slept alone.

Chapter 20

Day four, and for the first time in years, I didn't feel irritated because my cat had soaked my ear, and you know what, I missed that irritation. Downstairs, I placed her dishes in the sink and washed them. I took the tag off her collar and attached it to my key chain, the last vestige of her existence. 'Jinx, property of blah, blah, blah.'

Fucking cat.

I swore off ever becoming attached to another animal. It takes a year to make them shit in a box, and they survive a dozen years after that. Seems like a set-up for misery, and I felt miserable that morning.

I stopped by Albertsons and grabbed a pint of whiskey, a bottle of Baileys, and the biggest crap-black coffee their deli offered. Before I hit the parking lot, I'd poured half the pint and a bunch of Baileys into my drink. I was pretty sure I wasn't breaking any office rules. Last time I checked, I hadn't written up a policies and procedure against drinking before noon, or one for having sex on my desk, and if I had, I planned on violating one of them that morning.

I went to work in a fouler mood than usual, so foul, I could only hope the four college boys waited for me. Sadly, they didn't. When I pulled into my slot, Don pulled in beside me. I exited with my purchases and he eyed my hands.

"What the hell?"

"I'm kick starting my day, Don."

"I guess so, what's eating you?"

"My cat died."

"You're drinking because your cat died?"

"No, I'm drinking because my life is shit, and I have barely a day to make my shit not stink."

Don shook his head. "Just seems like you're going about it all wrong. You need to be level headed."

We came up alongside each other as we entered the alley. "Don, do you ever use aggression to get yourself out of a rut?"

"What do you mean, like hit something?"

I smiled. "No, I mean like saying, 'I'm mad as hell, and I'm not taking this anymore.'"

"I practice the art of balance, Dick."

For a guy who spied on everyone, balance seemed like an easy word to throw around. "Bullshit."

"I do."

"Really?" He piqued my curiosity. "Let me ask a question?"

"Fire away."

"You ever pee in the shower?"

"Excuse me?"

"You know, do you ever grab your dick and drain it in the shower?"

"Why would I do that?"

"You mean to tell me, when you're in the shower, and you have the urge to piss, you step out of the shower, and you go to the toilet?"

"Of course, don't you?"

I rationalized, "Balance would dictate you don't waste water our state doesn't have. Balance would dictate you use the water coming out of that shower head to rinse that pee down the drain."

He shook his head. "That's gross, Dick."

"Gross is not hitting the drain, but rather your feet. Try it sometime, if you can write your name in the snow, you can hit that drain."

"What's the point of your story?" He faced me like I'd wasted his time.

"Doing what's expedient is often times better than plodding through life. And gritting your teeth, saying, 'fuck it' and working mad is a better route."

I hadn't convinced that anal-retentive podiatrist, but he sure brought some sunshine into my morning. Watching him squirm over my Oscar Madison lifestyle cheered me up. We made it to the second floor, and although the city's finest had departed, the morose yellow tape across Stella's door remained.

"Let's do lunch today."

"Let's have lunch, Don, no more DO. That sounds gay."

"Dick, don't use the G word, it's not politically kosher."

"Then quit sounding like a faggot, and I won't call you gay."

You would have thought I shot the poor bastard. He stared at me like a monkey. "Really? That's your answer. Do you ever socialize in public? And if you do, are you ever invited back to anywhere you go?"

I unlocked my door, turned, "We'll discuss it over lunch," and I entered my room. The light flashed on my office phone.

Damn transfer must not have worked.

I hit the button and listened to my recordings. I rushed through Mrs. Howard, who must have gained a little more knowledge of the publisher, Two Princes, because she bawled about me not giving her a fair chance. Guess that little self publisher wasn't all they pretended to be. After that, my ex reminded me she meant what she said about selling her interest to that worm, Hunter.

Yeah, yeah, I get it, you figure you have me bent over and you want to shove it in as far as you can. Two can play at that game, dear.

The third call was Dee.

Gawd damnit.

She said it disappointed her I wasn't in and that she would contact me next week. "No!" I screamed into the machine. "Shit, piss, fuck. I need you right now." I plopped down into my comfy chair, only I didn't feel very comfortable. I dumped the rest of the whiskey into my drink, and pretty much drank straight whiskey with a splash of coffee and Baileys.

A cold chill filtered through the vents. Odd, it was never cold in my office. Someone must have had the air conditioning on during the night. I turned up my thermostat and you would have thought I'd broken it. The fan up beyond the ducts sounded like it'd lost a propeller and slapped against the metal. "Shit," I turned it off and decided to suffer through the cold. Anything topped the noise.

I called maintenance and received an answering machine.

That's right, the police said Eddy hasn't shown up for work.

I hoped I didn't have to worry about that little freak, but I doubted he had anything to do with Stella's death. I turned my attention to Hal. If Eddy couldn't be found, Hal needed to fix the fan.

I dialed the owner.

"Hello?"

"Hal, Dick here."

"Hey, Dick, what can I do for you?"

"Well, for starters, you can send that little weasel away and stop letting him tell you what to do."

"Good Lord, Dick, he's not that bad, and the truth is, he's pretty sharp."

"And all that's fine, except he's all up in my shit and that irritates me."

Hal had the audacity to offer me Stella's office. "All he wants is that interior office with that huge arching window. That room is the coolest room in our building."

"It's my nest, and he's not getting it."

"One way or the other, he probably is. If Muffin sells her shares to him, he's just going to room up with you."

"And I will make his life a living hell."

"I suspect you will, Dick."

I shook it off. "It's neither here nor there, I called for another reason." Hal grunted, and I continued. "Your fan is busted, can you come fix it."

"The ceiling fan?"

"No, the hvac fan."

"Eddy still isn't around?"

"He's your employee; you should have better knowledge of that than me."

"Very well, I'll send someone over to take care of it."

"Today."

"I'll send someone over this morning, don't worry. Hey, why the hell do you need the air conditioner on?"

"I don't, I want the heat. Someone had the air conditioner on last night. Probably the reason why the fan's broken."

"Give me an hour; I'll have someone on the roof to fix it."

"Thanks, and think about what I said about Weasel."

He hung up without resolving that issue, but at least the fan would be fixed.

Chapter 21

Those ducts carry sound. I didn't realize how much sound they carried until I heard the repairman open the hatch on the roof, followed by an "Oh Shit" that I'm sure every tenant but Stella heard. Whatever he saw didn't make him happy because it went silent. Don made his way over and burst in. "Did you hear that?"

"Yeah, it's the repairman."

"That didn't sound like your normal 'Oh shit.'"

I pulled myself away from my own investigative online search and thought about it. "What does a normal 'Oh shit' sound like?"

"You know," he gave a couple of renditions of disappointed 'Oh shits.'"

"And what was his?"

"His sounded panicky."

I supposed Don had a point. "Well, I guess that means it's going to take more than an hour to fix."

Don left but ten minutes later came back. "Cops everywhere."

"What?"

"Out front, ten cop cars."

I walked across the hall and stood at his window. "I'll be damned."

Don peered out with me. "I wonder what they want?"

"I'd guess your thought about the 'Oh shit' was right."

We faced off and shared, "Eddy."

Turns out we were right, and Littleton showed up in my office a short while later.

"Let me guess, you found Eddy?"

Littleton focused his beady little eyes at me as if I had performed some Kreskin trick or as if I knew more than I should. "How did you know?"

I sat in my comfy chair and enlightened him. "What do I do for a living?"

"Get on with it, Mr. Dillard."

"Well, I've read every possible scenario for crime thrillers you could imagine, and most of them horribly cliché, or worse, terribly written. My mind wanders to what could be, and right now what could be is our missing maintenance man is plugging up my fucking heater."

"Where were you last night?"

"Seriously? This again? Let's see, I spent time in the coffee shop, beat the crap out of a college kid, gave food to a bum, and buried my cat. Where were you last night?"

"Did you hear anything?"

"On what day? Because I'm assuming he's been up there since Stella's been dead."

"We haven't determined that yet."

"Come on, detective, it doesn't take a professional to know if a body is fresh. Would you like me to go up and look for you?"

He hesitated, I could tell he wanted to say something unprofessional, which, considering the law enforcement in our town, doesn't take much, but to his credit he waved it off and waddled out my office. I know they didn't consider me a suspect, Littleton liked busting my balls. I think he had a hard-on for me.

Don came in right after Littleton left and pumped me. "So, what did he say?"

"It's Eddy."

Don shut up, turned, and rushed out my office.

What the hell?

He returned with a plastic lawn chair and set it across from my desk.

"Where did you get that?"

"I bought it yesterday, my gift to you." He sat in it.

"I don't want it; take it with you when you leave."

He frowned. "Do I have to leave again?"

"No, hell, we aren't going to get any peace. You know the whole interrogation thing is going to start all over."

"I'm starting to feel like we might be in danger."

I didn't feel it. "I wouldn't worry."

"Why do you say that?"

"They were killed at the same time and whoever did it is miles gone."

"How do you know that?"

I leaned forward and moved my screen so Don and I had direct eye contact. "Whoever did this was surprised by Eddy, and then surprised again by Stella."

Don had three different shades of worry hovering over him, mostly his worry of being weak. "Are you sure about that?"

"I'm not sure of anything other than I agree with that Nubian officer when she said 'don't believe in coincidences when it comes to murder.' Two random unrelated murders did not take place in this building on the same night. Of that, I'm sure."

"What about the miles gone part, are you sure of that too?"

I rattled my head side to side. "No, I'm not; however, if it makes you feel better, I'll lie that I do."

"You think they were casing the place out?"

"Not if it was a burglary." Don's knee bounced up and down, his foot sprung from the toes. "Stop that, you're rattling my desk."

"Sorry, nervous habit."

"You have a habit of being nervous?"

"No," he missed my sarcasm. "I shake my leg when I'm nervous." He stopped and pressed me. "So why don't you think they cased the place out?"

"We have eight offices on this floor, and only four of them are occupied, one which is only occupied during the summer. If they cased it out, they wouldn't have wasted their time here."

"So you don't think it was cased first?"

"I didn't say that, I said they didn't case it out for a burglary."

"You think they were after something else?"

"If they were going through my place, they were going after something more than money."

"So do you think it was for something else?"

"I do."

"Like?"

"Maybe they wanted to scare me out of my office."

"That's kind of extreme, killing people for it."

"Yeah, a little too extreme, but so is paying half a million for a quarter of my business."

Don's eyes widened. "Yeah, that's a bit much?"

I scowled; how dare he dress down my wonderful business.

"Well, you did admit it yourself."

I winked. "Time to get to the bottom of things."

Chapter 22

Life took on less giggles and a lot more shit. My miserable five days had turned into something more life and death. I supposed I should deal with the elephant in the room. Did the attorney do this? Was he some fucked up spoiled psycho-rich kid who took his toys home when kicked in the nuts at the schoolyard? Maybe a different elephant swam in my pool, maybe four college boys lost their cool and decided to trash my office, got caught and disposed of the witnesses. Maybe Don was a bigger freak than I suspected. I still had to consider Dee; maybe I'd slept with Alex Forrest and didn't realize it; maybe Stella and Eddy were the rabbits in the pot. Shit, maybe this wasn't about me. One thing about terror, if you let it get the best of you, it wins. I had a whodunit. I also had a whydunit. As important as I considered myself, I knew I wasn't that important. Killing over something related to me, other than my assdickery, made no sense.

The clock raced up to ten, and I hadn't done anything productive toward finding my author, and the chances were I'd be pulling an all-nighter because any minute a little black spinner would enter my office and entertain me with her presence. I stood and started a small pot of coffee, enough for two. When I finished, I slid in my liquored-up portion, dumped the rest of the Baileys and waited.

Sure as shit, Officer Black tapped on my door. "Come in, sweety."

I waited by the pot, and startled her standing beside the door. "You look like you could use a coffee."

She sighed. "I could."

"Hope you like cream, it's already added."

"That's fine."

Styrofoam, what a crappy product. You have to have talent to hold it without crushing it, and it doesn't hold but a couple of gulps.

I handed her a cup. "Say when." She let me top it off.

Don hadn't taken his chair, and although I told him I didn't want it, at least I had something for Officer Black to park her ass in.

"Upgrading your furniture, I see."

"Just for you."

I sat across from her and raised my cup in salute. She did likewise, and when she lifted the coffee to her lips, she smiled and didn't crease a worry line as she took a drink.

"Interesting creamer, what do you call that?"

"Hair of the dog."

She took another sip. "You know that drinking in the workplace is frowned upon."

"I cleared it with my boss." I sat my cup down. "Besides, it helps get the stick lodged up the ass out."

"Are we talking about you or me?"

I liked her, damn, I really did. "I wasn't aware you had one lodged up there. Do you need me to check?"

"Careful, Mr. Dillard, tread lightly."

"Oh, call me Dick."

"I've called you that several times over the last two days, trust me."

I removed the veneer of chit chat. "As much as I'd like to carry this to its conclusion, I suspect you aren't here to ask for a date."

"This has turned into a much more serious situation."

"You mean to tell me Stella's head being removed from her body wasn't serious enough?"

"We have two victims who didn't die of natural causes."

"So how did Eddy meet his fate?"

"We aren't releasing that."

"As in, because you don't know, or as in, because you want to smoke out the killer with a slip of the tongue?"

"We know."

"That obvious, huh?" I studied her expression. "May I speculate?"

Officer Black warned me, "Speculate too well and you might become a suspect."

"Well, it's nice to know you don't consider me one now." I rolled my fingertips in taps against my desk. How much did I want to know? Hell, I wanted to know everything. "I'll take my chances."

"You're not going to confess or anything are you? I mean, I don't need to cuff you and read you your rights?"

She made me laugh. "No, and I don't believe you think I did this."

"So tell me, how do you suspect the maintenance man was killed?"

"Eddy was a man, not a big man, but a man. He wasn't a wimp—wiry, and if you were going to kill him, you were either a hell of a lot bigger, like me, or you had a weapon. The problem with beating Eddy to death is he would run; he wouldn't take on someone. He feared people too much. From Stella, we know a weapon was used. It may have been post mortem, but clearly the amount of blood on her walls didn't come from strangulation and a mere cutting off the head." I lifted my cup and saluted again. "How am I doing so far?"

"Keep going."

"Stella's body showed signs of overkill. Did Eddy's?"

She shook her head. "I told you, we aren't disclosing that."

"Suit yourself. I'm guessing Stella was shot to death and then stabbed repeatedly. I'll guess Eddy was just shot. And since you never found blood down here from anyone else—"

"How do you know that?"

"Because you were looking for Eddy as a suspect, not a victim, and you weren't looking for another victim." I continued, "As I said, because there was no one else's blood found, I'm guessing Eddy was shot on that roof." I watched as she drained her cup and motioned for more. Like a good host, I took her cup and made my way to the pot. As I crossed the floor, I asked, "So, did I do your job for you?"

"Are you concerned, Mr. Dillard?"

"Should I be?"

"I would be."

I didn't know. Maybe, who cared? Life is life, and if someone wanted to kill me, my office became a pretty stupid place to try it. "I'm not worried anymore. This place is probably safer than Fort Knox right now."

"Well, we will be making it safer; we will be stationed around the promenade tonight."

"Thank God you told me. I would be so embarrassed if someone caught me masturbating to internet porn."

She stood and finished her second cup with a single swig.

Damn it, I would have drank that if she had left a little.

"Is that for shock value, because I'm not easily shocked."

I stood and walked her to my door. "I don't suspect you are." I held the door open. "Will you be on duty tonight?"

"I will."

"Well good. I will make it a point to stay late."

She dismissed my remark with a wave of her hand. "You may get yourself killed one day looking in all the wrong places."

"I'll remember that." I watched her move down the hall. I wished they let women cops wear red high heels.

Chapter 23

I could hear their conversations as plain as day. "Gawd Damnit, get the blade out of his head." I assumed they meant the fan propeller blade. Geez, I hoped I hadn't cut the poor bastard up too bad. However, from the banging in the ducts, I assumed I had, because it appeared they had to go down the line to pick up Eddy's sliced-off pieces from when the fan had kicked on. I hoped they were thorough in cleaning up the mess. The last thing I wanted was the smell of decaying flesh when I turned on the heat, which I damn well expected to do sometime that day.

I drank the remainder of my alcohol-laced coffee. A thin layer of calm and pile of 'I-don't-give-a-shit' overcame me—always did when I drank. The sun hadn't entered the courtyard, and I sat and shivered my ass off. I set my phone to forward and grabbed my laptop. Hell with it, I'd conduct business in the coffee shop.

Outside my door, Littleton approached. "Dillard?"

I locked my door and turned. "Yes?"

"Where are you going in such a rush?"

"A rush? Do I look like I have my track shoes on?" I slung my laptop bag over my shoulder and scooted around the jolly detective.

He caught my arm. "I'm talking to you."

"Detective, it's cold as shit in that room. I'm going to go down to the coffee shop." I looked down at his hand. "And if you ever put your hand on me again, I won't care what your job is."

"I'm a police officer; I can do what I want."

"You better read up on your job description."

We stood opposite each other, and he released his grip.

"Are we done?"

He crossed his arms. "No, I have a question."

"Shoot." I winked.

"Did Eddy ever come to you for advice on writing?"

"Eddy? Hardly. I doubt he could have written on a bathroom wall." I thought about most authors. "But that doesn't stop people from trying to write a book."

"Doesn't everyone have a book in them?"

"No." I assured him, "Very few people have a sentence in them, let alone a book."

"Did you have many conversations with Eddy?"

"Rarely. Every once in awhile, he'd walk down the hall and check on needs, but as for personal conversation, hardly ever."

"Can you explain this?" He held up my business card.

"Well, I'm not happy with it. Wish they had used a heavier stock and the embossing is all fucked up."

He raised his voice. "I'm talking about the fact that this was in his pocket." He waved it in my face.

"Well, since your fingerprints are all over it, maybe I should ask you that question."

I'd irritated him. "Why would he have one of your business cards in his pocket if you and he never had a conversation beyond needs?"

"I have thousands of those, of which half go out to people who think I'm an asshole because I've rejected them. I suspect you can find my business card in random trashcans all over America."

"This wasn't found in a random trashcan, it was found in the breast pocket of a dead man."

"And that means what? Are you fishing?" I motioned for him to follow me to the elevator. "I'm reluctant to ask because I'm pretty sure of the answer; however, I'll ask anyway. Do you believe, in even a fraction of one percent that I had anything to do with the death of Eddy?" We stopped at the elevator, and I punched the down arrow.

Littleton sized me up. "I don't, but I think the death of Mr. Wilcox and Ms. Timmons are tied to the break-in of your place."

"Well, if that's the case, then shouldn't someone be worried about my wellbeing?"

"You want me to assign someone to you? I can assign you a bodyguard."

"I haven't been threatened. Seems like a waste of manpower." I stepped into the elevator and hit ground.

As the doors closed, he offered, "How about Officer Black?"

I stuck my foot out and caught the door. "On second thought, yeah, I'll take a bodyguard." I couldn't think of a prettier person to make fun of than Officer Black.

"I'll send her down to the coffee shop. Don't leave."

"Oh, trust me, I'll stick around for that cute little thing."

He pointed. "Don't harass her, and be professional, Mr. Dillard."

Professional, such an ambiguous word. I let the door close and made my way to the coffee shop.

Comfortable in Dee's spot, I enjoyed the mesmerizing of customers by the ten a.m. showing of the Hungarian Rhapsody #2 by Liszt on the promenade fountain.

I wouldn't have recognized Officer Black had she stood in a trance like all the rest of the patrons, but her movement caught my eye. She didn't pay attention to the music. She also didn't have on her uniform.

"Wow! You dress down really well." I reached out and poked her shoulder. "Except you are wearing your vest under that sweater, sort of gives you a thickness."

"Gee thanks, just what a girl wants to hear, that's she's thick."

I couldn't help but notice her sidearm. "Sort of conspicuous don't you think?"

She put her hand on the butt of the gun and patted it like a friend. "Deal with it."

I shrugged.

"Speaking of conspicuous, you sure spend a lot of time in this spot."

"My, my, you have kept tabs on me."

She smiled. "Not really, but I happened to like a good coffee, and I've seen you in here, in this spot, three times.

I explained my situation and how I needed to find the woman who could help me out of my financial woe.

"So that's why you have the 'Let's talk' sign in your window."

"About time someone didn't think it was for them."

"Well it wasn't so much the wording that clued me in. Orange giraffes aren't my calling card. Had you put a shark, I might have thought you were talking to me."

"Why do I get this feeling I'm going to be safe with you?"

She shot back, "Why do I get this feeling I'm not going to be safe with you?"

Chapter 24

"So this woman who you fathered a child with, what's she like?"

"I haven't any idea. I haven't spoken to her, outside of a phone call three days ago, in twenty years, and quite honestly, I don't remember talking to her then." I turned in my seat and realized officer Black hung on my words. "Say, what's your name?"

"Why?"

"Well, if you are plain clothed, shouldn't I be entitled to call you by your first name?"

"Ebony."

I stared. "Bullshit."

"Seriously."

"Your parents named you Ebony when your last name is Black?"

"They assumed one day I'd marry and lose my last name, and they wanted me to keep my identity."

"No offense, but your identity is written all over your face." I sat back and shook my head. "I don't think anyone would confuse you for Scandinavian if your name had been Solveig."

"Considering your name is Dick, and that no one would confuse you for anything other than a dick, you have little room to speak, Mr. Dillard."

"Touché, Ebony, touché."

Ebony asked, "So what does this mystery woman you slept with look like?"

I pulled her picture from my bag. "Here."

Ebony whistled. "Good looking woman. How did you wind up with her?" She found her dig cute.

"I have my moments." It dawned on me her intentions. "Don't suspect her."

"Why?"

"I might get lucky, and I don't need you fucking up my shit."

She handed the picture back. "I am moved by the eloquence of your words. You have such a grasp of the English language."

"I'm a man for all seasons."

"Oh, and I'm the season of truck driver?"

"Let's not kid ourselves E.B, if you hang out with other cops, my language isn't any worse, and I'm sure it's constructed better."

"I do, and it is, but I am a woman, and I sort of hoped this assignment would educate me in a broader vocabulary."

Did I get schooled?

Unbelievable, a woman, a police woman no less, just brought a flush to my ears as though a school teacher had punished me for speaking out of turn. "What would you like? Would you like me to get all sesquipedalian on you?"

"How about somewhere in the middle? If I have to carry a dictionary with me, I might start cussing."

"Fair enough." I wanted information about Eddy. I wondered if we could see any action on the roof if we moved. "Lunch."

Ebony balked. "It's only ten in the morning, I'm fine."

"I'm not asking, I'm telling. Since you are my bodyguard, you go."

"Very well." She stood and scanned the room.

"You're taking this job too seriously."

"Well, it doesn't hurt to look around and see who is either staring at us or avoiding us at all cost."

"So is anyone staring at us?"

"Not that I can tell."

"You're not very observant."

She turned and questioned. "Who is staring at us?"

"Far corner, by the door, little old lady."

"You mean the one who thinks a middle-aged white guy and a hot black chick being together is wrong."

"Yep."

"She doesn't count." We made our way through the café, and I tapped the table of the elderly woman. "She'd make a great daughter-in-law, huh?" I motioned to Ebony.

The woman scorned me with her pissant frown.

"Leave her alone, Dick."

We crossed the promenade to the sports bar and took a booth with a view of my building. An occasional policeman made an appearance high above. "How stuck was he?"

"They got him out easy enough, but some of him was still down in the vents."

"Some of him?"

"Well, apparently when someone turned on the heaters, the central fan cut him up. Took a hand and chunk of head."

I guess telling her I turned on the heater wouldn't make the story any cooler so I kept that information to myself. "Was he shot?"

"I'm supposed to keep that information a secret."

"Come on Ebony, you are protecting me because you think I might have been the target, which for what reason is beyond me, but I suspect you are aware of a hell of a lot about me, that I'm not the killer, and that I don't have a huge circle of friends. Who am I going to divulge any info to?"

She leaned into the booth. "It looks like his neck was broken. He didn't have any bullet holes or stab wounds, but he did have what appeared to be puncture wound from something other than a knife."

"And you have suspicions about my mysterious author? I might not have remembered sleeping with her, but last time I checked my ledger, I hadn't slept with any neck-breaking women."

"Might have been two people."

"Was it two people?"

She sat back. "What do you think?"

"I don't know, but the fact that you are suggesting it, I suspect when you guys did your investigation of Stella's office, and even as smeared and wiped as those prints were, you found footprints left behind, and you found two sets."

"You're scary good for a man who spent less than twenty minutes in her office, and I assume no time on the roof."

"As I told you before, I've learned a lot by disproving the shitty plots of a lot of shitty writers."

The waitress came by. Nice to know they didn't wear any more clothes during the day than at night, slick little shorts and a tank top so tight I could see the montgomeries on her areolas.

Ebony whispered, "Down, boy."

"That obvious?"

Ebony turned to our help. "What's your best salad?"

"I suggest the Cobb." She turned to me. "And you?"

"I suggest a Bloody Mary. Two; one for me, and one for my body guard."

"I'm not drinking at ten thirty in the morning."

I reminded her, "You've already had an Irish Coffee."

"And that was enough."

I held up two fingers to the waitress. "She'll drink it."

Ebony warned me. "One and one only!"

One means five.

Chapter 25

"Why would someone want you dead?" My bodyguard turned back into cop, investigating over my lovely bloody Mary.

"Don't."

"Excuse me?"

"Just stay pretty. Don't act like a detective. It's not becoming."

She tilted her head the way Muffin used to do when she found something I said unappealing. "Why is it when you say something to me it sounds overtly sexist?"

Her words stunned me. Could she be that dense? "Surely you've come to realize that your beauty is the most strikingly magnificent feature upon meeting you."

"And there's a lot more to me."

"I'm sure there is, but right now, getting a boner looking at you is all I care about."

"Oh—my—God. You are a pervert."

"I assure you, I am the furthest thing from a pervert. I'm up front and honest about what I think and feel. I'm not going to go home and dream about you. I'm not going to masturbate to you. It's not how I roll."

That shut her up.

I knew it would. I didn't need to discuss an investigation with her. If I needed information to crack who did this, I'd ask the questions.

She sat there wounded, as though my flattery had ruined her image of twenty-first century feminism. "Don't act indignant."

"You seem to think I'm nothing more than a pretty face. That's offensive."

"You are much more than a pretty face. You are a beautiful face and smokin' hot body."

I had reached her limit. "Just stop saying anything else. We can just pretend like neither of us is here."

I winked and saluted her with my drink. As the waitress breezed by, I mentioned, "Now, she's just a pretty face."

Ebony waved me off the conversation with a shake of her head.

I pointed to the barmaid. "However, that one is beautiful. Dare I say, a run for your money."

Ebony paused and gave my consideration some momentum. "Hardly."

"Ah hah! You do care."

"I do not care, but if we are now judging—"

"I'm only judging her against you."

"She's not that good looking. She has narrow eyes, and her chin is weak."

"She's not as good looking as you, huh?"

"That's not for me to say."

"Ah, but it is. You don't like that I think she's beautiful."

Ebony huffed. "Because she's not." She glared. "You're just trying to get under my skin."

"No, just under that sweater."

Her mouth dropped and she went doe-eyed. "Oh my Lord, you have just propositioned a police officer."

I considered that. "I don't think so. Yes, I am completely infatuated with you, yes, I'd like to lick your titties, maybe even nibble on them, but honestly, I'm not going to pay you for it."

"You wouldn't have enough money to shake my hand." If a black woman could turn red, she would have looked like a cherry. "Can we finish up and go?" She drained her bloody Mary as though sucking a cock.

I winked and waved the waitress over. "Two more, please."

Ebony objected.

"Oh come on. This is a paid holiday for you."

"You are no holiday, and if I could get away with it, I'd kill you myself."

There are times when I have felt the interplay between certain people, no matter how contentious, is delightfully and mutually satisfying. I suspected this was one of those times. "You don't mean that."

"I most certainly do."

However, for as much as she did protest that next drink, she sure treated it like a penis. In fact, I could see we were going to burn a few more hours in that joint. I suggested some games. "You want to play a round of darts?"

She rolled the salt off her lips with her tongue. "Don't tempt me with sharp objects."

"How about some music, you want me to play some Motown?"

"Oh, I get it, because I'm black, that's what I listen to?" She stood and pulled some quarters from her pocket. "Maybe I should see if they have any disco for you?"

"I like disco."

"You would, because you are old."

"Sit down, they don't have a jukebox."

"So you are just being a dick?"

"Pretty much." I informed her. "I'm not that old. I'll be fifty next year."

"And that's not old?"

"How old are you? Or should I say young?"

"I'm thirty two."

That surprised me. "I don't know if I should be disappointed or amazed."

"Why?"

"Because you don't have that many good years left on that body."

She pointed a finger, a well manicured, caramel-colored, nail-polished finger at me. "Fuck you, fuck you, fuck you," in slow drawn out rebukes.

"Well, that's a start." I smiled. "So, that's who I am, do you think anyone would want me dead over that?" I figured a flavor of Dick could help her better understand if I'd really be worth killing.

"Is this a shtick routine to you, Mr. Dillard?"

I shrugged. "A little bit. This is how I live, I'm not beholden to anyone, and I don't give a shit what people think. Politically correct is for bleeding hearts, and prayers are for rightwing sinners. The question is; would you kill me for it?

"Maybe if you slept with someone's wife?"

"Well, I haven't."

"Jealous boyfriend?"

"I haven't slept with anyone this year, and trust me a boyfriend would have begged me to screw the last piece of work I did screw."

"So is there anyone who benefits from your death?"

I couldn't help but be offended. Did she think I didn't already have that figured out? I used that worthless little mixed drink straw, the stirring straw—the one if you tried to suck through it, you'd have an aneurysm–to knock the salt off the rim of my glass. "My wife and a sleazy attorney tied to the building. Those are the only two who would benefit from my death. As much as I'd like you to lock up Muffin, I can safely eliminate her as a suspect."

"Why, maybe she would pay someone."

"Muffin? Hell no. Muffin loves money too much. She wouldn't part with it."

"Even if it meant making more?"

Muffin had the brain of a hamster. "Her ability to think beyond the box barely got her out of the womb."

"And the attorney?"

"He's a weasel. I don't know much about him, but unless he's a sociopath, there'd be no reason to kill me. He has me over the barrel, not vice versa."

"So where does that leave us?"

I smiled. Did she not know? I waved my hand to the barmaid and held two fingers up. "Another round."

Chapter 26

My phone rang. I recognized the number, Mrs. Howard. As much as I wanted to entertain myself with her begging, I didn't want to waste time when Ebony provided so much better entertainment.

"Business?"

"No, someone who doesn't know to let the dream go." I let it slip to voicemail.

"What about one of them?"

"Who?"

"One of your clients?"

"They aren't clients, they are submitters."

"All the more reason. What about one of them?"

"Can you really get pissed enough at being rejected to kill a publisher?"

"What are writers like?" Her detective spirit flowed through her question.

The definitive answer.

"Delusional, self absorbed, highly insecure, sure the world will end if you don't give them assurances they are the next fucking Jack Kerouac."

"And how many are the next Kerouac?"

"Well—" I looked to the ceiling and rattled off all the promising authors of that caliber. "One and I can't find her."

"Any that might find your rejections insensitive?"

"Why do you think I send them a form letter?"

She quizzed me on my wording and together we came to the conclusion that as painful as it felt to be rejected, nothing in my verbiage warranted death. "Besides, a man did this crime and guys don't call me to chew me out. They tend to write back and get it off their chest. Women call because they want to keep yapping. I don't know if it's because the pussy gets the best of them, and they think they can bottle it up and pour it on me, or if it's just something in their DNA."

Ebony threw her hands up. "You just can't steer a boat through calm waters can you?"

"What?"

"Hello, you're talking to a woman."

"Yeah, but you aren't a batshit crazy writing woman." I eyed her. "And don't play innocent, when all else fails, that Lyle Lovitt between your legs sings to men."

"Lyle Lovett?"

"He's ugly like a vagina."

She took me to task. "It is not an ugly thing. It's a beautiful opening to the reproductive cycle."

"It looks like a bulldog eating peanut butter."

Ebony raised her hand to the barmaid, "NUTHER!"

"Wow, did that turn you on?"

"No, I just need more to drink to keep me from fucking you up with my pistol."

"Well, it's good to know you aren't a mean drinker."

She scowled. "That remains to be seen."

I changed the subject. "So, when you said that Eddy was stuffed in the HVAC, do you mean they laid him in, or they packed him in?"

"Either way, someone with some muscle put him in. The opening is five feet high."

"Ladder?"

"Not that we could tell."

"Don't those vents have locks on them?"

"Someone came prepared. Bolt cutters."

I wondered.

"What are you thinking?"

"Nothing."

"Tell me. I value your opinion, Mr. Dillard."

"Call me Dick."

"Do I have to?"

"If you want me to respond, you have to ask for Dick."

"How about Richard?"

"How about I call you Candy?"

She sighed. "Tell me your opinion, Dick."

"I'm not accusing anyone of anything, and I seriously don't want to go there, but my friend and floor mate, Don, buys a lot of shit."

"You think Dr. Coleman could have done this?"

"I don't know. He's nosy as all get out, but, I don't know." I dismissed it. "No, he's not the killin' kind. He's the kind who would masturbate in private and feel all guilty afterward. Probably spend the night in confessional. He definitely wouldn't have come to work the next day if he'd killed Stella. He reeks of panic in a confrontational situation and would have sung like Brittany Spears' Oops song when Littleton questioned us."

"What about Mr. Thompson?"

"Harold? Have you seen Harold?"

"No, we can't reach him."

"That's because he and his wife Louise are in South Africa. They live there six months and here six months. He's a diamond importer." I stopped her reaction. "And he doesn't keep diamonds in his office." I continued. "As for him committing murder, he's so far into his twilight years, that his gray hairs are older than me. He didn't kill anybody, and if you met Louise, you'd know he has no desire in killing anyone. The fact he hasn't killed that dusty cunt means he's the most forgiving human on the planet. She makes Muffin look like Mother Teresa."

Ebony waited until I finished. "You make me long for the locker room conversations back at the station."

"You don't mean that."

"Yeah, I do, I really do."

"You like those schleps you work with? Seriously? A bunch of half trained monkeys we give guns to?"

"Those are my colleagues, Dick."

"They are donut-eating slobs with six months of training. They are a half step higher than security guards at the mall."

"What's that make me?"

I studied her lips, her eyes, her curves. "A smokin' hot black chick with cuffs."

She squeezed her eyes shut and tried to refrain.

I started to utter another line but she raised her hand.

"Don't. Don't say what's on your lips. Swallow it and take a drink to wash it down. Enjoy the ambiance, order us some lunch, hell, ogle at the barmaid, I don't care; just don't talk to me right now."

I believe she's starting to melt in my hands like hot butter.

Mrs. Howard called back and from the chirp of my phone, I knew she'd left a message. My steak held more interest, and I carved it up to inspect how rare they cooked it.

Nothing worse than gray steak.

I expected that bitch to moo when I stuck a fork in it.

The afternoon crowd consisted of clerks and middle management from the various trendy shops. Ebony and I stood out among pinstripes and power skirts. Listening to young adults with answers to the world's problems amused me. Behind me, a jack-off counted the ways the government screwed him on his paycheck.

Me, me, me.

When he didn't yap about himself, the douche-bag across from him stroked his ego with a slurry of muddy references about how smart he was.

"Leave it alone, Dick."

I turned my attention. "What?"

"I can see your wheels spinning. Just let them be."

"I don't have an issue with letting them be. I'd just like to let them know they are insignificant idiots."

"They may be, but do you remember when you were their age?"

She had it down.

Mid twenties, fresh out of college, out to set the world ablaze.

No one on the planet had my understanding of the world. "Good point."

As though her observation came home to roost, two cute little spinners from the perfume counter stopped by the boy's table

to let them know how appreciated they were. One young woman
said, "Gil, that presentation you gave on end-cap sales was spot on. I
was telling Helen that our movement of accessories was hindered by
lack of exposure."

Lunch time is no place for shop. Then again, talking shop
isn't always about business. I whispered, "You want to know just
how much I was like these boys?"

"Okay?"

When the two skirts made it out of ear shot, I counted down.
"Three, two, one—"

"Bet I can get her to suck my dick." Gilbert spoke.

Ebony shook her head and smiled. "How did you know that
was coming?"

"Because they are me twenty-five years ago."

"Oh Lord, another generation of Dick Dillards?"

"Looks that way."

"Now aren't you glad you didn't say anything to them?"

"No. Just because they act like I did, doesn't lessen the fact
that they're idiots. I was an idiot back then too, and I would have
bitch slapped the twenty-five year old me back to my one room
studio on the beach."

"You lived on the beach?"

"I had a mullet too."

"Wow, that's going to be a hard image to erase."

"Trust me, toss in the polyester and bell bottoms, that image
doesn't' get any better." I turned the tables. "What about you?"

"Graduated at the turn of the century, we were way past bad
styles."

"What did you want to be?"

"Everyone wanted me to be a model but I was too short.
Became a flight attendant for a couple of years, but had a bad
experience with a pilot."

"Harassment?"

"Not hardly, and I'm surprised you of all people would find anything wrong with that. No, he didn't mind having a black girlfriend as long as it wasn't in his hometown. I was his anywhere girl. Paris, London, New York, but when I showed up in his hometown of Boston his family had a cow, especially his wife." She frowned as though she missed the experience. "After that, he requested I be moved to another assignment and they stuck me in domestic and sort of treated me like I had stalked Phillip, so I embarked on a new career."

"A cop?"

"I thought about a prison guard."

It dawned on me, something didn't add up. "Wait a minute, you told me two days ago that your significant other was a woman."

"So."

"What are you, bisexual?"

"I tell every lecherous man who sizes me up that I'm lesbian, because anything else and they don't seem to care."

"Damn it, so much for converting you."

"Dick, you're really out of touch. You don't 'convert' someone who's gay. That's a rude thing to say to someone who is."

"Well, you're not so how is saying it to you rude?"

"Because I'm black, and I've felt like the outsider looking in. I know how they feel."

"Don't get your panties in a bunch."

I heard a familiar voice—four of them. I turned and saw my four college boys on their way to our location.

Ebony watched with interest. "Isn't that the fat kid who chased you?"

"Yes indeed." Behind him, three others marched on a mission; the last had two black eyes, cotton in both nostrils and a bandage over the bridge of his nose. When they reached our booth, the kid with the face of hamburger took his position in the front of the pack, his mates created a wall behind him.

He leaned over the table and had so much cotton in his face he sounded like a harelip, "No more fucking games. Either you step out with us and take your ass-whopping like a man, or we'll do it right here."

My elbows rested on the table, and I rubbed each bicep with my hands loosening them up. "You ever spend a night in jail, young man?"

"I don't give a shit. So far, you've assaulted me three times."

"And right now I'm in the company of this lovely woman, and I don't want to be disturbed."

He turned toward Ebony and then back at me. "Tell your nigger friend to leave."

The breath of his words had not reached my face before I had dislodged his hands and tilted his face downward to the table. With one hand I held my drink aloft and the other I caught him by the back of the head and guided his cheek into the edge of the table with a thud. His ass came to rest beside me, a wall between his friends. As they approached, Ebony pulled her shield from her waist and drew her gun. Everyone froze.

Ebony warned them. "I would suggest you four young men find the exit really fast. Because if I have to call this in, all of you are going to spend time in jail."

The young man in my charge wasn't getting off that easy. As he attempted to scoot out and leave, I put my arm around his neck and squeezed him like a lover. "I've got something I want you to do."

I put my drink down and wiped a spot of blood coming from his ear. "I want you to apologize to my friend."

He hesitated and I took a fistful of hair. I gathered it in, and like a facelift his eyes widened. I slid him forward and his chest came to rest on the table. "Real polite-like, and I want you to mean it."

"I'm sorry."

I questioned. "Sorry about what?"

"Sorry for calling you that name."

I leaned in. "What name?"

"Please mister, I don't want to say it again."

"No, I don't suspect you do with my dick half way up your ass right now, huh?"

"No, sir."

"How badly beat up do you have to be before you quit letting your friends talk you into this." He remained mute. "This isn't over, is it?"

We'd caught the attention of the manager who made his way to our table. "Is there a problem here?"

Ebony motioned to her badge on the table. "Everything is under control, and this young man and his friends need to be shown the door."

The manager bowed, and I released the kid. He slid from the booth and the manager escorted the four of them out."

"Thank you, Dick."

"Dick is good sometimes, huh?"

Ebony laughed, a belly laugh, the first time I'd seen her let loose. "You are a man through and through, albeit your own man."

"And you're still a smokin' hot black cop."

Chapter 28

"Are you okay to drive?"

"I'm fine." I slid out of the booth. "I have a police officer with me."

"I know I couldn't drive right now."

"Trust me, I have a little more density, I absorb well." Hell, we'd had nine or ten bloody Marys in three hours. "And I don't know what time you think it is, but it's not even one yet. We aren't driving anywhere; we're heading back to my office."

Ebony's eyes glazed.

"You okay?"

"I'd really rather not have my co-workers see me in this condition."

I noted. "They left an hour ago."

"I'm sure there's still a detail left behind."

"We'll take the stairs." We snuck up and found the floor empty, just echoes of our voices.

"Shh, I don't want anyone seeing me like this."

Like a woman, she couldn't just keep her mouth shut, and Don popped his head out. "Hey Dick…and is that Officer Black?"

I turned Ebony against the wall, and she blurted, "Frisk me!"

Don stepped closer. "Is she drunk?"

"A little." I held her up, pressed against the wall while I unlocked my door.

"Why?"

"Because she drank too much."

"No, why is she with you?"

"She's my bodyguard."

Don's face deflated. "You get a bodyguard? What am I, a red shirt?"

"They suspect my room's pilfering might have been the cause of all of this. They suspect I might be in danger."

"If you are in danger, then I'm in danger. You saw what happen to Eddy and Stella."

Fixing Don's spying would be easy. "If you hang out with me, you will be in danger, that's for sure."

Don did a quick scan up and down the hall and stepped back into his office. I could hear it lock and then the deadbolt click.

That a boy, Don.

"You ready, little girl?"

"Aye aye, Captain Dick." The last two drinks, which I tried to slow her down on, had kicked in. She turned and fell into my arms. I lifted an arm and dropped my other through her legs, and in an easy heave, I lifted her in a fireman's carry.

What a shitty fucking time to not have a chair besides my comfy. I didn't have the heart to put her on Don's plastic chair, so I sacrificed mine.

With her a minute from snoring, I ran across the hall and pounded on Don's door.

Nothing.

Chicken shit hid in there and played possum. "Open up, Damnit."

I heard the bolt twist and the lock snap. He spied out, a chain guarding the last vestige to freedom. "Yes?"

"I need your couch."

"My couch?"

"Yes, I can't set Officer Black on the floor."

With the reluctance of a whore taking a credit card, he hemmed and hawed.

"Give me your fucking couch, Don."

He slid the chain and let me in. I'd forgot he had two couches. "You were going to say no? It's not like I'm taking the only thing your lazy ass can lie down on."

"It ruins the ambiance with only one."

"Geez, you're a retard." I took note of the creepy posters of feet, models of tarsals and metatarsals, tubes of foot gel and antibiotics, thankful I only had to deal with shitty writers and not stinky-ass feet. "Grab that end." Watching Don lift the end of the couch eliminated him as a suspect. What a first-class pussy. He made us stop every four feet because the weight burdened him. Lifting Eddy five feet would have killed him.

We made it across the hall, and I felt like I should pay him to go see a proctologist to get the stick out of his ass. "Thanks, Don."

"Do you need help getting her to the couch?"

He had too much spirit in his question. "No, I can do it."

"You sure, because I can help." He showed more enthusiasm than I'd seen in the ten years he'd been practicing.

"I'm fine." I noticed we still had a chill. Not sure if turning the heat on would stink the place, and I suggested. "If you have a blanket over there, I'd appreciate it."

Don left and came back with two. "Blue or green?"

I shrugged. "I don't fucking care, just a blanket." I grabbed the green one.

"Are you sure, the blue would go with the room better."

"I'm not decorating, Don."

He bowed. "Very well. It's your room."

I escorted him out and locked my door. Lot of good that would do. I had a frosted glass window that anyone could break, and damn it, if they did, I'd be pissed. I liked that window; it was a classic and part of the original architecture of the building. The last door of its kind left.

I realized I had stuck us in that room. My shitfaced bodyguard wasn't going anywhere for awhile. I couldn't leave her alone; hell, I'd feel like a first class douche bag if I left, came back and she had her head somewhere other than on top of her smoking hot black body. I wrote my cell number on my business card and called Don.

"Friendly Feet Podiatry, can I help you?"

What a spastic name.

"Don, I need you to do me a solid."

"Solid?"

"A favor. Shit, don't you watch cartoons?" If he'd said no, I would have called him a liar. "Anyway, I need you to deliver my telephone number to the clerk downstairs, unless you are up to going to the liquor store for me."

"I can't, I have a client at three."

It was only one thirty but that anal shit wouldn't budge. "Fine then, come take this to him, it'll take two minutes and you can bring me back two coffees."

To my surprise, Don did it with only a minimal amount of bitching.

My phone rang. "Hello?"

"Someone gave me your card and said to call this number."

"Yeah, you're the kid who never leaves the café right?"

"One and the same."

"I'm the guy you want to trade lives with."

"Oh, yeah. How can I help you?"

"I'm right above you, room 202. I need two bottles of liquor: whiskey and something girly like Peach Schnapps. Also some chasers, and a two liter of Pepsi."

"Um, we don't sell that here."

"No shit, I need you to go buy it."

"Excuse me?"

"I'll give you a hundred just to do the dirty work, give me the receipt and I'll pay the rest."

"Why can't you do it?"

Ebony girly snored, looking more comfortable than I ever did, curled up in my chair, sort of like Jinx. "I've been asked by the police to not leave my office for my own safety."

"I won't get in trouble for this will I?"

"No." I learned a long time ago, 'please' doesn't have nearly as nice a ring to it as 'I'll give you a hundred.' My father taught me that one.

I hung up, walked to my chair. I reached down and cupped Ebony's knees under one arm and reached around her back with the other.

A feather.

Damn girl couldn't weigh more than a buck ten soaking wet, which I would have given a fortune to see. I carried her to the couch. As I released her, she let out a coo and rolled to her side. I carefully removed her side arm so she didn't kill herself accidentally.

Unbelievable, she's not even trained to feel it go.

I set it on the floor and put a blanket over her. I used a stuffed animal, one of my clients sent me, to rest her head. I hoped she didn't slobber on it.

"Sleep tight, young lady."

Chapter 29

The kid showed up, and I made good on my promise. I tossed him a C-note and two twenties to cover the rest. He peered over my shoulder and observed. "I don't think she's going to drink much.

Ebony slumbered somewhere between la la land and pukeville.

"She'll wake up and be good as new."

He noticed the print on my door. "I didn't know they had a publisher up here." His face lit up, and I knew the next words out of his mouth; however, the severity was worse than I thought. "I'm a poet."

A fucking poet.

I might have disdain for writers, but I hated poets, and unless your name is Maya Angelou, don't come to me with your drivel. Just because you don't have a story in you, doesn't mean you have thirty drumbeat lines instead. Leave the poetry between the sheets while you're trying to get that cute little red head in your sociology class to allow you to nibble on her labia.

"Yep, I'm a publisher." My voice dropped to a deadpan, and I sucked the air out of the room.

To no avail, he continued. "This is what I want to do."

"I thought you wanted to own your own business?"

"I do, I do, but I want to inspire a generation."

Holy shit, give this kid a vagina.

'Inspire a generation?' How old was this kid and what sort of pot did he smoke. Ten dollars said he played the guitar and lived with a woman who didn't shave. "That's a noble cause." I had to ask, and I knew he'd take it the wrong way. "Do you have much material?"

"Do I? Wow, do you want to see it?"

Fuck no!

I had no desire to see his poetry. "Tell you what, you find an editor, clean it up, write a cover and synopsis, and send it to me. I'll give you the same consideration I give all submissions." I wanted to tell the kid the pile of papers in the middle of the room amounted to my considerations.

"So when would you like it by?"

I think he'd already bought his Lamborghini. "Slow down. You have to take those steps first. Just let someone professional look at your work before you send it to me."

"Do you have anyone in mind?" He made himself a nuisance by inching his way into my office.

"Here." I went to my desk and pulled out a card of the editor I liked the least. One I knew would find me sending her a poet a rancorous move on my part. "Take this, she can look at your work," I warned him, "For a fee, but well worth it."

He held it to his face like a puzzle. "How do you pronounce the last name?"

"Don't worry about that, just call her Liz." I turned to the door and with a gentle sweep of my hand made quick order of our visit. "Don't forget to call her." I put an arm on the door and waited for him to side step out, knowing he wanted to ask more questions.

He read my name on the glass. "Thanks, Mr. Dillard."

"Glad I could help." I hadn't seen the last of him. "Hey, what's your name?" I knew to ask since he'd made us best buds.

"Jerry, but my friends call me Slam man."

"Slam man?" Which I wasn't calling him in this lifetime.

"I duel at a lot of poetry slams."

I had to remain still as a mantis because to shake my head in disbelief would have been rude. "I see." I smiled. "Well, Jerry, do yourself proud and get Liz to look at that work."

"Thanks, Mr. Dillard." He moved down the hall with a lighter step and a happier beat.

Glad I could help.

Not that anyone considered him a suspect, but I could check him off the list. That kid didn't know what I did ten minutes earlier. Now he'd take a bullet for me, and I suspected he'd be reciting one of his soliloquies as he did.

Behind me, Ebony hadn't moved. Nice to know she wasn't a kicker when she slept. I hated kickers. Muffin kicked, kicked like she had epilepsy. There were times I wanted to strap her down, but then I'd have to listen to her incessant whining about being restricted. She hated having too many covers on her, a leg or arm over her; even Jinx bugged the shit out of her. Man, I felt sorry for that sad-sack husband of hers.

I brought up 411 on my phone. Asked for the nearest pizza joint and laid in a call.

"Hello"

"I need a couple of pizzas."

"What's your address?"

When I gave it, the kid said, "Hey, weren't there two dead bodies found in that building this week?"

"Yep, but I'm not one them, so send me a pizza."

"Just a minute, sir." I could hear him arguing with someone in the background.

Another voice picked up. "Hello, sir, this is the manager."

"Okay, is there an issue with me ordering pizzas?"

"Well, it's just that we're short staffed and my driver is spooked to deliver a pizza there."

"It's the middle of the fucking day."

"Still."

"Tell that little weasel piece of shit to get his ass over here."
The phone went dead. Damn it. My second attempt went better, but
the truth was, I wound up ordering from the shitty place, the place
with pizza made of cardboard. I had them put so much crap on those
pizzas they were salads on crust.

When they arrived, by the driver's eyes, our place had gained
local attention. "Aren't you a little scared to be in this building?"

What the hell had the media told people, that ghosts did
these murders? "It's three in the afternoon, should I be?" Odd how
all the tenants in the building carried on business as usual.

"I know I would be." Scared or not, he stayed long enough to
get a tip.

As he headed to the elevator, I said, "Be careful, they said
they snatched them right from the elevator."

He spun around and hurried to the stairwell.

"They found a head in there."

He paused, caught between the only two options afforded
him.

"I'm just fucking with you. There are police all around, you
are safe, and it's broad daylight."

He scurried to the stairs.

I turned back to the room, and the drift of onions, peppers,
sausage, bacon, and tomato sauce had sent Ebony into a trance. She
bounced up. "Pizza!"

Chapter 30

"I see I have all my clothes on." Ebony sat up and twisted her sweater so it draped properly. "Where is my gun?" Her panic elevated to high alert.

"Relax, it's at your feet."

"How'd it get there?"

"I kind of thought it discharging while you were lying down might be hard to explain to your boss."

She shrugged. "Thanks."

"You're welcome."

"How long was I out?"

"Two hours." I handed her a Brain Hemorrhage.

"What is this?"

"Coffee, Tia Maria, Peach Schnapps, couple of other things."

"Seriously? Is this what you do all day?"

"No, but since I have company, I wanted to make the most of it."

Ebony sipped a little, hesitated. "Not bad actually. Better than those Bloody Marys."

"Cheers!" I raised my whiskey coke. "Here's to hair on your chest."

She hesitated. "Really? You want to see that on me?"

I grinned. The thought had no appeal. "For a cop, you are a light weight."

"Is drinking a prerequisite for carrying a badge?" She shook her head. "If so, I'm so off the force." She pulled a leg under her butt. "Hey, where'd the couch come from?"

"You don't recognize it?"

"Should I?"

"If you're a good detective you should."

My chocolate bodyguard rubbed her hand over the back of the couch. "Clean, un-scuffed, Dr. Coleman's office."

"There's hope for you yet." I retrieved an aspirin from my desk. "Here, take this before we start another round, it'll keep the hangover at bay."

Ebony palmed the pill and tossed it in her mouth. Lifting the cup, she stopped. "What's happening to my drink?"

"Oh! Shit, forgot to tell you. Drink quick, it curdles."

"Oh my God, it looks gross."

I smiled. "It looks like a brain hemorrhage."

I took it from her and chugged it. "I'll make a smaller one, in a one swallow size." I handed it back, and she downed the aspirin. "Thanks."

"So you want to take me to the roof?"

The cop in her hesitated. "No, I'm still drunk, and I'm sure I have colleagues up there."

"How about after some food?"

She nodded. "Maybe."

"I need to get up there."

Ebony didn't wait for me to invite her to dine. She lifted a lid and leaned over the box. "Is this our plate?" I'm sure she knew I didn't have kitchenware, after all, she drank out of a used Styrofoam cup.

"I guess that's why I got two." She laid her box over her lap and would have given poor Don a coronary eating on his furniture. I pulled my comfy around and rested my feet atop my desk, a bridge for my box to sit.

"So why do you need to get up there?"

"Well, no offense to your crack staff, but I suspect I'm every bit as good a sleuth as they are."

Ebony disagreed. "Doubtful, they have the finest tools in the world."

"It's not about tools, it's about the moment."

"The moment?"

"Just get me up there."

She soaked up enough carbs to balance out the high. Thirty minutes and she felt like a teenager whose pregnancy test came back negative. "Any gum?"

"Of course." A man who drinks for breakfast always has gum. I roiled my desk for some Doublemint. Damn stuff was the 'nasty' of the three flavors, but wiped out liquor breath best. "Here."

"Bathroom?"

"Right over there." I motioned to the south.

She made her way over my papers and into the void that hollowed out the rest of the office. "You have a lot of space here." Her voice echoed in the emptiness.

"And I like it vacant." The thought of anyone else sharing my space pissed me off.

Ebony closed the bathroom door behind her and shouted, "Wow, you're cleaner than I expected."

I had a few quirks; a spotless bathroom was one of them. I hollered. "Thanks."

Fucking WOW!

She returned without her sweater and vest, just an undersized white tee shirt minus a bra. I had underestimated those tits. They stood to attention like ground hogs in heat, nipples you could hold hangers on. A poster of Farrah Fawcett all over again. I zeroed in on that chest. "So you don't think you might need a bra?"

"Oh come on, Dick, you wanted to make sure there was no hair on my chest, right?"

I had an erection and no words to think of, so I bowed my head and pointed to the door. We made our way to the stairs, dark, the rooftop path unlit. A soft glow from the lower-floor lamp.

"Looking up at that door would have been dark as hell." I led us to the roof. The door opened in and we had to back away, only one person could stand on the platform as it opened. "Wait."

"What?"

"Trade places."

I had her take the lead, and I stood on the first step. She opened the door.

"Something's wrong."

"Why?"

"This door would have been locked. Eddy would have been where you are and the killer would have stood on this step and waited for him to unlock the door."

"And?"

"How tall are you?"

"Five-two, maybe three in these shoes."

"I'm six-five, and I can barely lean far enough forward to control you as you open that door. Eddy was probably around five-eight. To control him, the killer would have to be six-eight at least."

"Why would he have to control him?"

"Eddy would have run."

Her voice bounced off the corner of the stairwell. "Maybe he did, but on the roof, where would he have gone?"

"He would have gotten away, and I know why."

Chapter 31

We walked out onto the roof, a large flat plain that overlooked the promenade on one side and the street on the other.

"So why do you think Eddy would have gotten away?"

"If the perp didn't have a gun on him, Eddy would have been smart enough to run to that corner, to that funny looking thing over there." I pointed to a vent that looked like a limp penis."

"What is that?"

"It's a dorade box." We made our way to the contraption.

"But it has a screen on it?"

I reached over and snapped it off. "It pulls right off."

Ebony peered down into the darkness. "Where's it go?"

"It's a heat relief for the elevator motor. It worms its way down about six feet and drops into the motor room." I offered. "Eddy showed this to me once when I was up here poking around, and this would have been on his mind if he had to run."

"But he wound up in the HVAC vent, could he have become confused?"

That humored me. "No, there's no confusing these two," I slapped the round tube but motioned to the big square HVAC box. "He got stuffed in that one after he was killed."

"So he never made it here, why?"

"We know that from my leaving my office to my returning, it was probably dark when the killer led him up here." I backed up the way we came. As I did, I had to avoid a piece of rebar sticking up out of the roof. A few yards further and I stepped over a ledge. I stopped and wondered how many feet stood between the ledge and the rebar. "Where was the puncture wound on Eddy?"

"Right about here." Ebony rubbed the side of her stomach.

"Come here."

She stood alongside me.

"If you tripped on that ledge at a dead run, how far forward do you think you would sail?"

We knelt down and studied the layout of the roof. "I'm guessing over the top of that bar." She stepped over the ledge and inspected the rebar. "There looks like blood on it."

"So good of your team to notice."

"We studied the area from the door to the HVAC."

"As I said, it's about the moment, not the tools."

"So it is."

"That's your reason why Eddy didn't make it. He impaled himself on that bar."

Ebony turned to me. "The shops were still open when this happened. You would think he would have screamed when he hit this bar. Shouldn't someone have heard it?"

"Doubtful, with all the noise from the fountain, people laughing, busy shoppers. Not to mention, he would only have screamed for about ten seconds before his killer caught up to him. I doubt Eddy screamed much after the guy broke his neck." I hesitated. "Although, the alley is pretty shielded from the promenade, someone there might have heard a scream."

Ebony sighed. "People coming and going, I don't know how we could even locate someone who might have been in that alley at that time."

Looking at her tits made me lose my focus. I wanted to reach out and rub the end of a nipple, maybe even blow on it and see if I could make it stand any more erect. "What?"

She turned, "I said, finding someone who heard a scream would be hard, besides, they'd just be confirming what we already know."

"But they'd give us a time of death, and with the cameras in the garage, maybe a chance to see a nervous traveler."

"Again, finding anyone who may or may not have heard a scream, who happened to be in that alley at that moment, is a needle in a hay stack."

"How long have you been a cop?"

"Four years."

I shook my head. "You should have done porn. I think you would have been better at that."

I'd set her off. "Excuse me."

I had a hard time taking her indignation seriously, she put her hands akimbo and her chest sprang forward.

"Don't they teach any of you cops to be aware of your surroundings?"

"What are you talking about?"

"How many times have you walked that alley?" I turned to the exit and waved her to follow me.

She caught up and paced me. "Maybe twice."

"What did you see when you were down there?"

"Garbage."

"Nothing else?"

"There are no cameras down there, trust me. I pay attention to my surroundings."

"You do?"

"Yes I do."

I stopped her. "Close your eyes." She smiled as though I tried to pull a fast one. "Just close them." When she did, I asked, "What color underwear are you wearing?"

She slid her eyes open and reached up to my neck, pulling me toward her so she could whisper in my ear. "That's easy...I'm not wearing any."

Fuck.

That backfired. I whispered back, our faces inches from each other, me staring at those big beautiful dark eyes. "Well, how about this. Without turning around, how many flags are flying over the promenade?"

"Damn it," She huffed, "I don't recall any."

I turned her around and a promenade banner flew from each corner. I straightened. "And they let you carry a gun. Gawd damn our world is fucked up."

"Dick, I'm sort of offended by that."

"And I'm offended you didn't notice a bum living in the alley next to one of the bins."

"There's a bum down there?"

"And furthermore, he's one of your citizens. You really need to pay attention and get to know the meek in this world." I opened the roof door and waited for her to pass. "His name is Tom, pretend like you like him."

Chapter 32

Behind a blue dumpster, Tom read a book. He probably read more that day than the average freshman in college. Hard to understand what happens to a man when he loses his way. What separates us and makes the journey so hard. I couldn't speak for Tom, I didn't know his story, but not every bum wound up there because of drugs. Some can't cope in this world. Hell, if not for a lucky break here or there, I might have pilfered the garbage bin with him. The lines on his face told a story—one of torment, deep creases of worry. His cheeks sunk in, probably from a lack of teeth. He studied the book with precision. Tom could read, and he could read well. He had uncanny concentration. We stood and waited as he turned a page and his briefness with each one impressed me.

"Hey, Tom." I didn't want to startle him, so I called out before he looked up.

"The fightin' man!" He dismissed his book and stroked his beard. "Who's the lovely lady?"

"I'm Officer Black." She flashed her shield and crossed her arms. "We'd like to ask you a couple of questions."

He frowned. "I thought you weren't going to bring the police?"

I raised a hand. "She isn't here to hassle you. We just need to know if you heard anything the other night."

"What night?" He rolled to his knees and struggled to get up. I didn't realize, but he appeared crippled. His right leg didn't bend. As he came upright, he listed heavy to his left. He exhaled, part relief, part exhaustion. "Okay, how can I help you?"

Ebony didn't flinch when a wave of urine, decomposing food, and sweat floated past us, but I sure as hell did.

She asked, "Can you remember back a few nights ago?"

"The night Dick got into the fight in the alley?"

She turned to me with a bit of motherly contempt. "Yes, that night."

"Those boys started it."

"It's not about that."

Tom tilted his head and shrugged. "What else was there?"

"Did you hear anything strange?"

"Like what?"

"Someone screaming for help."

He took his index finger and tapped his temple. "Trying to recall what night it was I heard something up high."

"Something up high?"

"Sounded like it came from one of them rooftops."

I interrupted, "About what time?"

"Not too long after you left."

Poor schlep had been still alive. Shit, if I'd stayed longer, Eddy wouldn't have wandered down an empty hallway. Isn't that just how timing works?

"Did you see anyone race through this alley like they were in a hurry?" Ebony stepped closer.

"Everyone races down this alley. It's not the most inviting place."

She offered, "No, I suppose it isn't." Ebony thanked him. I could see her instincts as a decent human being kick in. Her lips pursed and angst swam over our leaving.

She whispered, "He's going to be okay, won't he?"

We worked our way back to my office. "I suppose that's relative, don't you? I mean, he's been out here for at least three days, and he's made it this far."

"Maybe I can get him help?"

"Careful there. A lot of homeless don't trust help. The caveats sometimes come with bars."

She gave Tom a look over her shoulder. "I suppose, but maybe we could see that he gets some new clothes, shoes, blankets."

"You're fighting a losing battle. What he needs is permanence, not a holdover."

She sighed and pushed the second floor button and the doors closed. "The killer must have been still in Stella's office."

"Looks like Stella was killed first, not second."

"Dick, there's still something not right."

I thought one step ahead of her. "Why the overkill on Stella?"

"Exactly."

"Stella may have been the intended target, and my office something completely separate, and if that's the case, maybe you are back to square one on my office. Maybe fate would have it that two separate crimes really did take place that night. If so, we need to find the person who broke into my office. He may have seen Stella's killer."

"Or might have been a third victim?"

I hoped another dumb shit wasn't stuffed in some crevice somewhere in our building. "Something tells me he's just fine. I think I spoke to him after the fact."

"Anyone you'd like to share with me?" She took my arm, and we exited into the hallway. "Let's go in and discuss this over another drink."

I started to have a permanent hard-on for this girl. She spoke my language. "Officer Black, I can't think of a better thing to do on a Thursday afternoon than to drink with a cute young thing like you."

"Don't get too amorous, we are collecting information."

What a buzz kill.

I opened the door and waved her in. She made her way to my desk and helped herself to a pad of paper and a pen. She started jotting down things at a feverish pace.

“What are you writing?”

“A timeline.” She tucked the pen over her ear. “So, who do you think broke in here?”

“A little pencil-pushing fuck-up.”

She paused, studied my face. “A certain attorney?”

“One and the same.”

“Do you have more than suspicion? I can’t bring him in on your detesting him.”

“I don’t want him brought in. Let’s see if we can get him back over here.” I went to the air conditioner and turned down the temperature. It wasn’t warm, but I sort of wanted to see what her nipples would do if I lowered the room five degrees.

Chapter 33

DeBussey's Suite Bergamasque: Clair De Lune trumpeted through the walls.

"Shit, doesn't that unnerve you?" Ebony brought her hand to her chest.

"No, it feels like a cuckoo clock." I stood and went to the window. My drawing and sign still taped for the outside world to see, hopefully a certain author had noticed. Down below myriad shoppers stopped and tuned in the dancing sprays of water. "It's now four."

"Shall we see if the attorney will pay you a visit?"

I liked the way Ebony thought. You'd have figured with as cute as she was, boys would have kept her on her back and away from thinking. "I'll give Hal a call and tell him I want to see his attorney about a deal."

"He might be too afraid to come."

"No, he's a cocky little shit, he thinks his daddy can protect him."

She nodded at my phone. "Let's call him then." She had a naughty look, like she had just blown the school principal.

I couldn't help but enjoy this side of Ebony, I just didn't know which one of us planned to play good cop if he arrived. I called Hal and gave him some bullshit story about reconsidering the attorney's offer. It pissed me off that Hal had an air of relief in giving me that jack-off attorney's number.

I put the call in, Jim, Jim Hunter answered. "Hello?"

"Mr. Hunter, Dick Dillard here."

"What do you want, Mr. Dillard?"

"I suspect I might have been a bit rude to you the other day."

"I guess those hours are ticking away. Panicking a little are you?"

I wanted to reach through the phone and choke the little bitch, but I waxed on-waxed off and went to a happy place, the imaginary grave of my ex-wife. "Yes, I'd like to work something out. Can you meet with me?"

"I don't know, Mr. Dillard. You were sort of threatening when I last was there."

"Well, Officer Black is here, and she will be more than happy to mediate."

He perked up as though curious of my activity. "You have a police officer there?"

"Just for my protection with the murders and all." He stood on a precipice and I needed that little rat to jump. "Trust me, this will be more beneficial than giving my ex half a mil."

I'd hooked him. "I like to hear that."

"Say five?" I winked to Ebony.

"Five thirty, I'll have to wrap up business here first." Little fuck probably busied himself wiping his grandpa's ass. The only business he had was cleaning toilets. His greed had the best of him and he stammered with excitement.

"Excellent." My phone beeped. I pulled it away and saw Mrs. Howard calling. "I have another call, so I guess I'll see you around five thirty."

"That you will." He cackled like the kid who'd won a fight.

I clicked over to the other line. "Hello, Mrs. Howard?"

"Hello, Mr. Dillard." I recognized her husky voice. I don't know how many cigarettes that woman smoked in her life but it'd given her a Bette Davis voice that had to grate her ex-husband's nerves to no end.

"Why are we still in concert?"

"What?"

Dumb bitch.

"Why are we communicating?"

"Are you ready to take me on as a client?" She had a smugness that I didn't understand.

"What possibly do you mean? We've already had this conversation." This is what I hated about writers. Once someone tells them they are ready for the publishing world, they can't accept that perhaps the kind gestures of idiots, who hadn't a clue, treated them to lies. In her case, whoever had told her she was ready for the publishing world should have been taken out and executed for gross negligence.

"Two Princes told me they spoke to you, and I was to call you?"

Well, those bitches at Two Princes played it well. Nice job.

"I've not spoken to anyone about you. Honestly, you haven't come up. If I'm being honest, Mrs. Howard, you need lots of work. Go out and find a critique group, an online critique group like Writers World, a good editor, maybe a writing class or two, perhaps a writing boot camp, and study." The dead air between us led me to believe she'd hung up. "Mrs. Howard?"

"What?" She shouted loud enough to catch Ebony's attention.

"Wasn't sure if you were still there."

"Are you telling me that Two Princes never contacted you?"

"Who is Two Princes?"

"My new publisher or was my publisher."

"So what happened?"

"She wanted me to pay all my own expenses. She wasn't a real publisher, not like you, Mr. Dillard, and when I confronted her, she said she'd spoken to you and that you wanted me back."

Great, now a half-baked vanity press pawned clients my direction. What the fuck was the publishing world coming to? "I can promise you, you've been lied to."

Mrs. Howard started bawling, sounding like a dying toad. Damn, what meds was this woman on. "Calm down, Mrs. Howard."

"So will you take another look?"

"No, but it's not the end of the world. Take my advice and trust me, you will be ready one day."

"Very well, Mr. Dillard. I'll let you go. I'm sure you'll see it differently when I'm famous."

"I might, but let's cross that bridge when we get there." I had to give her credit, she wouldn't go down easy.

Crazy hag.

I disconnected and smiled. "So, drinks before Hunter gets here?"

"How about you drink the Hemorrhage, and I'll drink the whiskey coke?"

Wow, she might be sleeping on the couch again.

Chapter 34

Ebony left the office to hit Don up for a favor. She came back with glassware and Don in tow. I'm pretty sure those tits, showing like a wet tee shirt contest, helped persuade him to tag along.

"I've brought some company and nicer accommodations for drinking." She handed me a glass. "Pour!"

Don waved his hand. "No, it's not closing time and I might get a late walk in."

Ebony stopped him. "Nonsense, the day is as good as done, and you need to relax." She handed him a glass. "Give him a hemorrhage."

She suspected what I already knew; Don couldn't handle a man's drink.

"What's that?" he peered into the glass.

I smiled. "Nothing too harsh."

"Why so little?"

"Well, it won't last long in that state, and if it turns into the next state, you'll understand the name."

He sniffed it, the peach and coffee gave it an unusual, but bouquetish aroma. "Doesn't smell bad."

Ebony offered, "Doesn't taste bad either." She lifted her glass of whiskey, having not yet put coke in it, and saluted. The two of them clinked glasses and downed their drinks. Ebony's cheeks tightened. She might think she had tough resolve, but I could tell that swig wanted to come back up.

"You might want to chase that quickly."

She nodded, and her eyes welled up. In a voice full of breath, she pushed out, "I think you're right." I handed her the coke and she drank straight from the liter. Somehow, sloppy seconds from her lips didn't bother me. Took moxie, I'd give her that. "Slow down, I don't mind you falling back to sleep, but I'd prefer you not heave on Don's couch."

Don stiffened. "Don't sit on the couch if you feel sick. I just had that couch professionally cleaned."

That was the most anal thing I'd ever heard him say, and he said anal shit all the time. Who professionally cleans a couch? Gawd damn, Don had a stick up his ass. "Don't worry, Don. If she should puke on your couch, I'll buy you a new one."

He protested. "That's not the point." Standing in the center of the room, he proclaimed all things, big and small, are about order, and order is derived from planning. I poured him another Hemorrhage. It was time to create chaos.

Fifteen minutes later, we had Don singing about what a shitty life he had, and how he wished he had bigger balls to do the things he really wanted to do. I'd dislodged that stick. He reminded me of a guy who desperately wanted to be part of whatever crowd would accept him. Don followed people. How he'd survived this long without doing something stupid someone suggested was beyond me. Somewhere in that life of his, someone must have told him to do something which caused stitches.

"You have any scars, Don?"

Six two-ounce drinks in him, a tipsy Don shook his head. "Damn it, excuse my French, but gosh no, I haven't done anything worthy of a scar."

"No bike crashes?"

"Oh, heck no. I always made sure I had my helmet, knee and elbow pads on."

The thought of him as a child alarmed me. I would have taken his lunch money. I am sure Don would have hated me if we had grown up together.

Ebony laughed. "You must have been a trend setter; little kids didn't wear helmets back in your day, did they?"

He nodded. "Thank you, yes, I was. Mind you, I took a razzing, but thanks to precautions, I am free of any broken bones, no stitches, hardly a bruise to speak of."

Mother fucker is proud of that?

I sat in my comfy and gazed at Don's delicacy. Ebony paid attention, but behind her smile her face cracked with amusement.

Ever the police officer, she worked her way to a few pertinent questions. "So, you said you heard Stella screaming in her room the night of the murder?"

"Yes."

"Did you hear any other voices? A man's voice perhaps?"

Don's face stressed over his answer. "I'm not sure."

Ebony pressed. "What do you mean?"

"I heard another voice, but sort of a feminine male voice. Not the kind of voice you would have thought was having sex with her."

"So you thought they were having sex?"

"I'm pretty sure they were."

Ebony patted the seat next to her, and Don sat. "Did you get a chance to see this mystery client of hers?"

"No, but I will say this. I think he was heavy."

I sat up in my comfy, interested in how he deduced that. Ebony continued. "Why do you think that?"

"Because he walked heavy."

"Heavy?"

"He creaked the floorboard. I could hear him walking across her office."

If Don was correct and the killer was her rendezvous, he'd eliminated every one of our suspects. Not a one of them had that kind of girth, except…me; however, my voice ranged several octaves below feminine.

Chapter 35

We'd liquored up Don to where he might puke on his couch. "Don, let me help you up and to your office."

His head bobbled. "The party is over?"

"Yeah, we have a visitor due in five minutes."

Don put his finger to his lips. "I'll be quiet."

"As much as I'd like to have you here to have my back, I think it's best if I do this alone."

His eyes widened, and he whispered, "Do you want me to take her with me?"

"No, that's okay."

"Are you sure? I'd watch her for ya'."

I took his hand and pulled him upright. I steadied Don and worked our way to the door. He turned and promised. "I will return when they leave."

Ebony smiled. "I'm looking forward to it."

I moved Don to his office, plopped him onto his couch and locked him in. If a killer roamed out there, no need to put Don in harm's way. I heard the elevator open. Out stepped four people.

Gawd damn.

That boy was right, his sister did look like him, and it proved my point; he'd make a damn fine looking woman. I could only guess the other two were Daddy and Granddaddy. I stood outside my office. "Hello, Jim, Jim Hunter."

Like an a cappella group, the three men said, "Hello." Ah yes, senior, junior, and three.

"I haven't had the pleasure." I turned all my attention on this blonde creature with them, dressed in a power skirt, the scent of Obsession, and eyes of cold steel.

She held her hand out in a limp gesture, as though she wanted me to kiss it. "Honey, I only kiss asses, not hands."

Her pleasant smile disappeared. "I see you are everything my brother said you were."

"Oh, I'm much more, trust me." I motioned to the three men. "You don't share their name as well do you?"

"No, I'm Jamie."

Fucking inbred lot.

"You're Jamie?" I turned to her father, "Wait, let me get this straight, your father's name is James, your name is James, you named your son James, and you then named your daughter Jamie?"

He barreled into me. "You have an issue with that, Mr. Dillard?"

"It's fucking weird." If they couldn't see that, heaven help them.

The senior member of the group stepped forward. "I can see you are a man who doesn't mince words. I like that. Perhaps you and I would be more compatible."

I looked at his progeny "The fact that you didn't stop that idiocy, I'm not sure how compatible we are, but you do sound like a more rational version." I waved them over. "Come in."

Ebony's eyes widened when she saw more than the runt of the litter. I could tell she wanted to run and dress.

"Don't worry about it, E.B., you look fine." I noted her presence to Jim senior. "The absolutely stunning looking woman on the couch is Officer Black; she's here for protection, your grandson's. She going to make sure I don't kill him."

Jim Jr. stepped in between me and his family. "I don't know who you think you're speaking to, but I will have you removed and placed in jail, along with your half-dressed cop if you lay a hand on my son."

Junior was the tallest of the group, but he still missed my height by seven inches. I narrowed the gap between us. "You step out of line, and I'll toss you out my window." I'd answered my own question; clearly, Ebony would be playing good cop.

She stood and raised her voice. "At ease, gentlemen."

Poor Jamie had shrunk behind her family. I had no idea how that little flower would make it as an attorney; maybe she could do porn lawsuits.

With his family in the room, and feeling every bit the man his father must have encouraged him to be on the way up the elevator, Jim, Jim Hunter made his debut. "You said you wanted to conduct business. If that's indeed the case, then let's do so. If not, then I guess we will see each other tomorrow." He pulled his father away and met me face to chest. "Which is it?"

I peered over the top of his head and asked his grandfather, "Are you aware your grandson broke into this office?" Granddad and I communicated. We didn't say anything to each other, but our eyes spoke volumes.

"I would think it's best if we don't say anything, Mr. Dillard."

"Look, this isn't a court of law, and it isn't a police interrogation. That boy of yours is going to squeal one way or another, and I'm sort of hoping it's the other, because I'd really like to beat it out him. However, I'm going to give you the opportunity to tell your piece-of-shit grandkid to tell me what I want to know. I promise you, I don't give a shit about what they were looking for. I know they didn't find it." I pointed out. "They didn't steal anything."

He turned to his grandkid. "Is this true, Jimmy?"

Junior tried to interrupt, but Granddad had enough sense to shut that dumb cunt up. He raised his hand and silenced Junior. "Is it true?"

"No—"

Everyone, including that deer-in-a-headlight sister knew he lied. "Don't lie to me, Jimmy."

Ebony offered, "You've not been Mirandized, nothing you say can be used against you. And you have three witnesses who would probably lie if we tried."

I'd had enough playing nice. I caught the pipsqueak by the throat and backed him up against the wall. "I need to know what you saw that night. Did you see anyone in the hallway?" I lifted him up so his loafers dangled off the ground.

He coughed and held onto my wrist to ease the tension on his neck. "I sent someone else."

I dropped him, and while he tried to gather his dignity, I turned to his father. "I suspect the old man didn't know, but something tells me you did."

I took a step toward junior, and he cowered. "Our contact never came back."

Chapter 36

Shake enough cages and you will find singing birds. "What were you looking for?" I pressed Junior.

Ebony tapped me. "Forget that."

She was right, what we wanted was information on a killer, but fuck it, I had other issues as well. "What were you looking for?"

"Isn't that obvious? We wanted that original contract."

I found the idea of a contract maker trying to steal a contract, as though that would make my lease null and void, comical. "The risk of ruining your careers over this office? That doesn't make sense." Something churned inside the patriarch. "What says you, Senior?"

"I say they should have had a little more faith in me." He smiled.

That old bag-of-shit figured out what they were up to and didn't want to talk. Must have been a hell of a profitable reason.

"Get on with what you want to know about who they hired. Listen to your police friend."

Ebony engineered the rest of the investigation. "You said your contact didn't come back. Have you heard from him?"

Jimmy had found composure and spoke for himself. "No. The last message was that he was inside and searching the place for what we were looking for."

"The contract, right?"

Jimmy nodded, "Yeah."

Gawd Damn it.

Something didn't measure up. They did not look for a fucking contract, and his hesitancy proved it. The more agitated I turned, the more nervous that little twit became.

Ebony put her hand on my bicep. "Relax, big guy." She continued. "What did he say, exactly?"

"After telling me he'd check every nook and cranny, he said someone was coming and he needed to hide."

"Did he say how he knew someone was coming?"

"He said he heard someone coming down the hall."

Ebony turned to me. "Heavy steps."

I suggested, "Could have been me. Maybe he hid in the bathroom."

Jim, Jim Hunter and I squared off. "What time did this conversation take place?"

He had shut me off and must have thought Ebony would save him, he only answered to her. "Seven fourteen."

"Dick, would that have been you?"

"No, I didn't get there until a little before eight."

Ebony focused on the break-in. "Did your man break the door open?"

"No."

"How did he get in?"

"He…" the weasel stopped. "He didn't break in."

I stepped in. "He didn't break in because he had a key." The fear on that attorney's face spoke volumes. I approached him, and he tried to move over to his family. I cut off his path. "Hal gave you a key to my place, didn't he?"

"I plead the fifth."

I slapped him alongside the head. "This isn't court, you moron."

"Okay, okay, don't hit me. Yes, Hal gave me a key. If you weren't such a fucking asshole, maybe you would have more friends."

"You mean like you? Let me count your friends." I ticked off the other three people with him. "I don't see them helping you, and your other friend is missing. You better worry about your own behavior." Little faggot had pushed me to the limit.

Ebony put all her five-two body in my path and rubbed her tits against my stomach. She peered upward. "Let me handle this. Go sit in your chair."

I retreated to my comfy and made sure the Hunter clan knew if I had to get out of my chair again, it would be to kick that midget's ass.

I poured myself a whiskey.

Junior pointed. "Should he be doing that in his condition?"

Ebony shrugged. "Probably not, but do you want to take it from him?"

Jamie worked her way around the men and came up alongside my desk. While Ebony conducted business, this blonde little spinner with a runner's build, stuffed in fishnets and pumps, asked, "Is that a bottle of peach Schnapps, grenadine, and Baileys?"

"It is."

"Wow, hemorrhages, my favorite."

I bet she had on a garter belt and a shaved pussy in a V. I served up a small amount.

She grabbed the bottles like a bartender, made it look like a brain, filled it to the top of the glass and pulled her jacket off. With the garment discarded, she pulled me up out of my seat and camped her ass against the lip of my desk. A drink ready for launch, she whispered, "Let's watch her crucify my brother."

Chapter 37

"What's the name of the person you hired?"

The senior Hunter stepped in, and the crafty veteran shut the others up. "At this point in time, with him missing, we aren't at liberty to give his name."

Ebony nodded. "I understand."

I didn't. "Wait a minute."

She turned and motioned for me to settle down. "So, Mr. Hunter, why can't your grandson give us the name?"

"Well, you've developed quite the mess lately, and our involvement wouldn't be good for practice. If our client should be located on your premises, well, let's just say, we don't want the association."

Ebony smiled. "So if we should find someone in a less-than-upright position, that wouldn't be your guy?"

Senior winked. "You got it, officer."

That was pretty much it. We'd dicked the dog with those four. The one good thing sat next to me. She gave the musty room a million dollar aroma, and if she'd have leaned over just a bit, I could have copped a view of her chest. Doubtful she had nipples like Ebony though. Not to mention, her tits were perky, which is never a good sign if you want substance. They would have had plenty of room to maneuver in a B cup.

She turned to me and pounded the shit out of that drink. "One more before the three amigos want to leave?"

"You better hurry, I'm about to toss them out."

She winked and poured herself a healthy dose. She also refreshed my glass of whiskey. With a nod, she held the glass up. "Bottoms up!"

I suspected the next time they broke into a place it'd be a twelve-step program to bail that little princess out.

"Come on, Jamie." Her father insisted. "Don't play with Mr. Dillard."

I whispered to Jamie, "Tell your brother if he really wants to be my partner that you and I are going to play spin-the-bottle—a lot."

She cooed, "Mr. Dillard, you are a dangerous man."

"In fact, make sure your father knows what my plans are."

She stood on her tippy toes and pecked me on the cheek. "You're sweet, no matter what they say."

If I were a betting man, I'd say Ebony wanted to pull her gun out and shoot Jamie. Her head swiveled, following Jamie as she met up with her family. "E.B!" I gained her attention. Ebony had a bout of the bitch in her. "It's all good."

She exhaled, and my damn erection came back. As ripe as that little Hunter was, she didn't have the magnetic appeal of that little piece of licorice. Ebony scolded me. "Nice to see you're entertaining the troops."

Women; good friends with each other until a man comes between them. If I'd had a tub, I'd have put mud in it and paid admission to see those two go at it, then I'd have washed them up for being dirty girls.

Ebony stepped back and joined me at the desk's edge as the Hunters filed out of my office. "I don't know what you're thinking, but whatever it is, you have shit on your grin."

I lowered my view. "I do, don't I!"

"You can wipe it off any time."

"Jealousy doesn't become you."

"Jealous? Me? Hardly." She elbowed me. "You think their associate is on the grounds?"

I folded my arms and nodded. "I do."

"Any ideas where?"

I continued nodding and concentrated on my door "Pretty sure where."

Ebony folded her arms and nodded as well, joining me in my view. "Want to tell me?"

"I'll take you there." I poured a glass of whiskey for me, and one for her. "After a drink."

"Put some coke in mine, please."

Yeah, I saw that coming. "Those straight shots aren't sitting well with you?"

She shook her head. "No, not really." She was honest, what a great quality.

"Let's take Don with us."

She pulled away from her drink. "You think he's awake?"

"He had twelve ounces of pussy drink; I should hope to God he's awake." I finished my whiskey, and we made our way to Don's office. I knocked and could hear him groaning. "Unbelievable, he's got a hangover."

The door clicked, and he opened it. "What?"

"Let's go, we have a mystery to solve."

"I don't feel good."

I pushed my way in. "You feel a little drunk, but you aren't that drunk. You had twelve ounces of liquor an hour ago. Now do a jumping jack and pump some blood in you."

Like the moron he was, he started to exercise.

"I'm kidding." I handed him a stick of Double Mint. "This'll freshen you up."

"High in sugar—not good for you." He countered with a stick of sugar free bitch gum.

"Whatever does the trick."

"How long have I been out?"

Ebony lifted her wrist and counted off the minutes. "According to my watch, less than an hour."

He circled around to his desk and pulled out an air mask. With a quick breath, he shook his head. "Ready."

What the fuck?

"What the hell was that?"

"Nitrous."

"Nitrous? You're a foot doctor, why do you have nitrous?"

He shrugged.

No wonder he couldn't handle his liquor. "Let's go."

"Where to?"

"The roof."

Chapter 38

The three of us exited to the roof, the last rays of sunlight danced on the horizon, an orange glow over the Pacific Ocean, beyond the promenade walls and city streets. Southern Cal could turn summer in the middle of spring, and that night had turned into one of those times.

Don insisted. "I don't want to see the air conditioner."

"We're not going there, don't worry." I hadn't told Don what sort of mystery we tried to solve. He hadn't been brought up to speed that we searched for a third victim. One had been enough for him. I'm pretty sure he had cried and sucked his thumb for the last few nights after we saw the headless corpse of Stella.

Don stayed clear of the HVAC and went over to the other side of the roof, over by the dorade tube. We followed him. "I thought you were going to check the air conditioner."

"I didn't say that. We need to check something else." Ebony and I stopped in front of Don who leaned against the tube.

Don pointed to a fly on the tube. "Oh look. These are the prettiest flies. I used to love seeing these as a kid." He directed us to a bright metallic green fly.

I saw another, and Ebony didn't say a word. I whispered "What do you think?"

She let out a soft shrill whistle. "Blow flies."

Don nodded like a school girl. "That's what they're called?"

I enlightened him. "Yes Don, they are called that. They also like to lay their eggs on meat."

He didn't register my remark and continued nodding his head like a song played inside that vacuum between his ears. "I see."

Ebony motioned to the vent. "Don, open that vent would you."

He gestured to the dorade vent. "This one?"

"Yeah."

Don unclipped it and several flies exited. "Oh wow, that's stinks."

"Bet the heat of the elevator has done a number on him."

Don dropped the vent. "No! Shoot. Is that smell what I think it is?"

I shrugged. "I don't know, what do you think it is?"

"You guys know. Look, I can't deal with another dead body, especially if we know them."

I calmed him. "We don't, don't worry." I motioned to Ebony. "That was quick. We didn't smell anything earlier today."

She whistled. "Gives us a rough time of death."Ebony sighed. "Shit, let's call Littleton."

"Let's wait."

Don screamed, "What for?"

"If the attorneys know their man is dead, they will shut up about why they were in my office. I might be able to get some information from this corpse."

Ebony agreed. "Yeah, they definitely didn't try to find a contract. They were after something else."

Don rationalized. "What about the poor dead guy?"

I shook my head. "He's not going anywhere, besides, if I hadn't said anything, he'd be there a hell of a lot longer." I asked Don. "You have paper gowns or sheets or something like that?"

"Sure, but why?"

"We need to find out about this guy."

"I'm not helping you pull him out. That's gross."

"We don't have to pull him out. We'll go down to the motor room and open the vent. He'll fall out." However, even I wasn't going to like that job. "I need something to wrap him up in."

"Can't we just call the cops?"

"Hello, what am I?" Ebony raised her hand.

"I mean, can't we have him removed tonight?"

I assured him. "Tomorrow." I worried Don would hyperventilate, or worse, lose sight of why we didn't want the cops to come in, and make the call. I would have to babysit that wimp the rest of the day. "Call your wife and tell her you're going to be working late."

"I have to stay?"

I chided him. "Wait, you are always wanting to hang out, and now you don't? Put your big-boy pants on and live a little. Who knows, you might get a scrape or two before this is all over."

"I seriously hope you aren't suggesting I might be in danger?"

"God, you are such a pussy."

We met back at the motor room. Don retrieved the paper liners from his patient room and we opened the vent. The heat had done a number on our victim, but for the most part, only being dead a couple of days, he wasn't in too bad of shape. Don stood by as Ebony and I retrieved a cell phone, wallet, and the contents from his pockets.

"You know, I could get in some serious trouble from the department if they knew I was doing this." Ebony had second thoughts.

"Hang with me."

"Don't worry, I'm already in this now."

When we finished, we wrapped up the victim to mummify him and slow some of the decomposition. We closed off the door and locked it. The stench and sweat from the heat left Ebony whining for a shower. "Sorry, E.B., but I don't have a shower."

Don intervened. "I do."

I felt slighted. "What you mean you do? How the hell did you get a shower?"

"It wasn't that hard, I had Hal's father plumb it in before he retired."

"How come you've never told me that?"

"I have, but you never listen to me."

He had a point. I made it a habit not listening to Don. Most of what he said, a fourth grader wouldn't be interested in.

"Bless you, Don." Ebony kissed him on the cheek.

Again, the erection. There it is, hard as a rock. Damn it.

I called out. "I've got dibs on seconds."

Chapter 39

What I wouldn't have given to have soaped up Ebony. I'd have scrubbed her like a dirty girl. Sadly, I waited my turn, and when I stood under the shower, I twisted to cold to keep from busting a nut right there under the jets.

Don pounded on the door. "Hey, don't use up all the hot water."

Yeah, yeah, it's not like he dealt with the corpse. He could use a moist towelette from KFC to clean up what dirt he involved himself in. "Hold your horses, unless you want to come in here and shower with me."

No response.

I don't think he considered what a thorough job I do scrubbing backs.

By the time I finished, the night had taken hold, and the artificial lighting of the promenade glowed amber into my office. The power of clean flesh radiated off Ebony, and if she was pretty before, she was beautiful now.

She had a towel wrapped around her head and put her hand to her chest. "What?"

I turned away. "Nothing."

"I thought maybe washing away my mascara scared you."

I hadn't noticed but played along. "Something like that." I winked.

She tossed me our dead guy's wallet. "Here, not sure what we can glean from this."

"What about the cell phone?"

She came alongside me and displayed his logs for that night and beyond.

"That second to last one is Hunter's. I suspect he died shortly thereafter. I wonder who owns this last number?" That final call lasted fifteen seconds. "He left a message on the last call."

"How do you know?"

"Logical deduction, the call is fifteen seconds."

I scanned the rest; one number came up once a day. "Home."

"Why do you think that?"

"Every call is at eight thirty, about the time a child would go to sleep. He has a small child. He calls to tuck him or her in."

"That's kind of a leap. Maybe he has a boss he checks in with."

"He's a freelance, probably a client of Junior's."

Ebony shook her head. "How are you coming up with that?"

"Think about it. No power attorney is going to put his trust in a third party. You can't get blackmailed by the actual killer, after all, possession is nine-tenth of the law, but you can get blackmailed by a supplier."

Ebony faced me like she wanted to fuck my brains out. "You are scary good."

"Let's see what happens if we hold down the one button." I put it on speaker phone and half a dozen messages were in the queue. "Larry, got your call, what the hell's going on over there, you sound like you're getting mugged. Call me back." The next call brought the truth that no matter how nefarious a man's activities turn out, inside us all is home. "Honey, are you okay. Are you working late again? Please let us know." The next three were the same woman's voice, and the sixth was a little girl asking why he hadn't called to tuck her in."

Ebony bowed her head. "Poor sap."

"Jack-off shouldn't have been prowling. My father used to say, 'nothing good happens after midnight.' Kid or no kid, he's responsible for his own behavior."

Ebony frowned. "Tell that to the kid."

I didn't have time to worry about the fatherless kids of this world, and honestly, that man may have tucked his little girl in at night, but sooner or later, he would have proved to be a shitty example of a parent. Maybe now his widow could go out and find a real husband; one that locked the doors at night before he tucked his family in for real and went to his room to give his wife a clitoris cleaning. "Tell his kid that her dad was a criminal."

"Whatever. She doesn't deserve that kind of pain."

"And that's his fault."

She changed the subject. "I noticed our attorney never left a message."

"Of course not. They can claim any call he made to them was a wrong number." I gave the phone to Ebony. "Be a cop. Call Larry's friend and press him for information about what he heard."

"If he knows Larry for who he is, why would he talk to me?"

"Be honest. Tell him Larry's dead."

It was worth a shot. Anything else and his suspicion would take over, and he would hang up.

Ebony placed the call "Hello, this is Officer Black of the L.A. Police Department…no, you aren't…I have some bad news about an associate of yours, Larry…" she picked up his wallet. "Harris. We found him deceased tonight…Because you were his last number…" She shrugged and started to doe-eye me. I rolled my fingers to keep going. "You aren't in any trouble, far from it. We want to solve this."

She listened for a minute. I died to hear what this zit head said, and whatever he said, Ebony nodded in victory.

"I just want to know what you heard in the voicemail." She listened again.

It dawned on me that Ebony had as attractive a voice as she did a face, and our caller had a boner. He would try to stretch this all night and sing during every second of that call. My urgent rolls to continue turned into rolls to finish.

"Okay, did you hear a voice?" She nodded. "You did…you don't say…I see." She tried to break in on his ramble, squeezing in, "That's enough, let us see what we can uncover. You've been a great help."

"So, what did he say?"

"Feminine male voice, and that the man was big, because our Larry, said, 'Holy fuck, he's tall.'"

Chapter 40

"Have you considered that your mysterious author, what's her name?"

I flinched at Ebony's implication. "Dee."

"Dee, might be short for Daniel, or David, or any other guy name?"

"E.B., I got a boner over her picture. Do not tell me she is a dude." I walked to my desk and retrieved her photo. "Does that look like a dude?"

Ebony turned on my desk lamp and studied the image. "Could be if you take all that make up off.

"And the tits?"

She warned me. "I've seen drags who look pretty damn good."

"What about the kid?"

"Dick, that could have been a ruse. He might have sent someone here to check on you."

"Don't say he, he is a she. I slept with her, and the last time I checked, no one I've slept with in all my years has had a cock and balls."

Ebony turned her attention to me. "You don't even know if you actually slept with this person. She said you did, and you bought into it. Also, this photo could be anyone."

I gathered myself. "Not buying it."

"Why?"

I paused, considered the manuscript. "Because of the work."

"What does the work have to do with it?"

"She knew intimate details."

"Like what?"

"That I'm not a small man if you know what I mean."

Ebony shrugged. "You're white, that's debatable."

"Wow, that's racist."

Her mouth hung open. "Seriously, coming from you, you are going to cast aspersions on me?"

"That's just racist."

"But probably true."

"You are no better than I am." I viewed the photo another time and exhaled. "This is no guy, and if this is indeed my mystery author, this is not our guy."

"Do you have a scanner and fax machine?"

I chuckled. How absurd was that? "Look around, do I look like I'm twenty-first century?"

"Dick, that's twentieth century stuff." She shook her head.

"Don has one. He has everything."

She snagged the photo from me and scooted across the hall. A few minutes later she returned. "There, we'll see what the office can come up with."

I shrugged. Good idea. I needed to know more about her so I could locate her. The most inept police department in the country should be able to find her. "I hope they come up with something. Did you give them her name?"

Her face dropped like I belittled her. "What do you think?"

"Okay." I backtracked. "I thought we were going on the assumption that the killer's intended target was Stella?"

"We'll get around to that. I just want to clear your plate first." Ebony grabbed her pad. "Who else?"

"The four boys, but it's not them."

She wrote it down anyway.

"My wife and her husband, and I could only be so lucky if they were the perps." It delighted me to see her jot the names down. "Don."

"Don?"

"You asked for all possible." I pointed out. "I'm a possible." I spread my hand to her. "You and Littleton are possible."

She didn't write any of those names down. "Anyone else?"

"Hal and Jim, Jim Hunter, but we've ruled out Jim."

"She reminded me. "We're looking for someone tall."

The reality was I didn't know anyone the height we might be looking for. My lone question mark was Dee, and if Dee Hallorin was the killer, she had an accomplice—the young woman who claimed to be my daughter, something I didn't want to believe, because I liked the idea of having a daughter. I assumed I'd never have kids and that depressed me. Hell, what could be better than one I sired who had already reached adulthood. No changing shitty diapers, no dealing with fucked-up reports cards, no having to kill some boy for sticking his dick in her. Shit, I seriously hoped that kid was mine. The worst part of having kids had passed with her.

"Neighbors you might have pissed off?"

"Mrs. Oliver."

"I was thinking more along the lines of big men with high voices."

"Maybe Mrs. Oliver is in drag."

"Is she big?"

For a ninety year old, she's fair height. Maybe five six."

"Dick, please be serious."

"I don't know anyone. I'm not much into high pitched men. I don't do gay."

"That's sort of rude to say that about someone."

"Sort of like calling my dick only big by a white-guy standard?"

"She tilted her head and softened her expression. "Oh, I'm sorry, did I hurt your feelings? Are you having a hard time letting my comment go?"

"Yeah, laugh it up."

"Nobody cares, so keep it in your pants."

Huh, she'd brought me back down to earth. The foreplay was nothing more than locker room banter. She knew how to get the best of me, just admit that our tension amounted to nothing more than fun and games.

"Okay, let's consider Stella?"

"What's to consider?"

"Was she ever married?"

"Divorced."

"Was her husband a big guy?"

"Yes he was." I thought back. "Extremely tall."

"High pitched voice?"

"No, normal dude. Just big." I questioned. "You guys had to investigate him. Don's remark about size had to set off bells and whistles when they located her ex."

"I'm not on the investigation team, Dick. I'm a foot soldier. I'd love to get out of my blues and do that; and solving this would help."

"Well, I'm sure your investigators have checked up on him." I reminded her. "They've been divorced longer than I have. He's never said boo to her."

"Have you ever had any interaction with him?"

"No, not really. Whenever I tell someone I'm a publisher, they invariably get around to telling me they have a story in them.

He was no different. He would always kid me that one day he was going to hit me up to look at his manuscript, but he wasn't serious."

"What's his name?"

"Ah fuck. Why don't I pay attention to people who bother me? What the hell was his name? He went by H.T., that's what everyone called him."

Chapter 41

I'm not going to lie and say I wouldn't have slept with Ebony if she'd pulled me on top of her and slipped my dick in her, but in reality, I didn't see that happening. She flirted well, better than a hooker looking for a tip, but when Don showed up and wanted to hang out, the bantering stopped. I didn't mind, nothing worse than frustration, and that's where my night headed.

Ebony peeled the towel off her head, her hair carefully held its perm. She turned and faced Don. "Hi, Don."

"Okay you two, I'm prepared to try one of those brain thingies again."

Ebony retrieved the bottles and must have paid attention when Jamie made hers, because she made it look like a brain. "Here you go, Doctor."

Don glowed. Being called doctor always gave him an erection. It's why I called him Don, no need to fan the flames. "Thank you, my lady."

Oh Lord, please.

I didn't want him going all Renaissance on me. "If you're going to hang out with us, I hope you'll be normal."

"You, my good sir, are the abnormal one."

I nodded, "Of that I'm sure." I treated Don like a third wheel, as though he didn't exist, but he did exist and thankfully, when I said, "Damn, I should know Stella's ex-husband's name." He answered.

"Howard."

I turned. "Really?"

"Yeah."

Ebony had her cop radar signaling. "Do you think the man with her that day was him?"

"Maybe. I told your boss it could be."

She continued. "You say maybe like maybe not, why?"

"I kind of heard his voice. Granted, it was muffled, but it didn't sound like Howard. This person had a higher voice."

"Like a woman's voice?"

"I don't know that I would have called it a woman's voice, more like a feminine guy's voice."

I interrupted. "You mean a gay voice?"

"If I were politically incorrect, I might use that term."

I cocked my head. "As opposed to what, queer?"

"You are incorrigible, Dick." Don wagged a finger.

"Yes he is." Muffin's voice slid in from the night as she and Charles entered.

I sneered at Don.

Fucker didn't lock my door when he came in.

"Why are you here?" I poured myself a drink, something Muffin had come to understand as the only way to tolerate her. "Chuck, can I interest you in a Muffin-numbing drink?" Poor bastard had to spend his twilight years with that cunt.

He declined and remained quiet, but Muffin had plenty to say. "I wanted to come by and find out if you are any closer to buying me out?"

"Oh yeah, I have a half million dollars here in my desk, but I want to roll around in it before I hand it over."

She eyed Ebony in that tit revealing shirt; contempt bubbled over. "Looks like you have company to roll around with."

"Have I introduced Officer Black?"

Muffin didn't miss a beat. "Is that a stripper's get up?"

Ebony stood. "Mrs. Dillard, I would caution you on what you say."

"Oh please, honey, don't call me Mrs. Dillard. I haven't had that horrible name since this wonderful gentleman," she gave Charles attention, "rescued me with a new name." She stepped forward and offered Ebony advice. "And if you are a police woman, you should dress more appropriately."

Besides withholding that dusty pussy from me, and her constant nagging about how much I brought home, I realized what I hated most about Muffin McCready was her meanness. I'd heard people say we were meant for each other, but nothing could have been further from the truth. I lived my life saying what I felt. Muffin, however, thrived on being a cunt. She wanted to belittle people to their face. I survived a dozen years because I knew how to piss her off, and she couldn't beat me—until that snaggletooth attorney of hers. He not only beat me, he took pleasure in entering through the backdoor. "How did you know I was here?"

"I thought the sign was for me, Dick."

Why did everyone think I wanted to talk to them? "The giraffe? Trust me, if I'd put a sign up for you, it would have been a stinky clam."

"Enjoy it while you can, Dicky. I'll see to it that you have a new business partner at five o'clock tomorrow."

I sighed, sucked down my drink like water, and turned to Ebony. "Is there anything you can arrest her for?"

Ebony felt sorry for me; she smiled but the air had gone out of the room. "Sorry."

"Come back tomorrow, Muffin." I waved her off, but I didn't have the authority to make her leave, she owned a quarter of the business. "I'm busy trying to secure the money."

She scanned the room, stopping at the bottles. "Yes, I can see you are deep in strategy." Muffin worked her way to Don. "Donald, why do you sit in company with him?"

"It's wonderful seeing you, Muffin." To Don's credit, he knew the difference between Muffin and me. "You look as radiant as ever, and your hair appears to turn more red every time I see you."

I offered. "You have to color the shit out of gray to get it to stick, that's why it so red."

"I do not color my hair."

Charles' expression turned zombie. If she was going to lie, she shouldn't let her husband stand in the room. Her words petrified him.

"Lift your skirt and let me see your front porch. I'll bet money it looks like the Golden Girls."

"Why do I bother with you?" She turned and demanded Charles to follow. "Tomorrow, Dick." She stomped out, and Charles bowed with forgiveness.

"Softly on the door, Chuck."

Don held his drink up. "She's not changed a bit."

"And that ain't a good thing, Don."

He shook his head. "No, it really isn't."

Ebony handed me another drink, and poured herself one. "Now that that is over, can we get back to business?"

I wet my lips with whiskey. "What did you have in mind?"

"I keep wondering why the attorneys tore this place apart."

It had bothered me all day, much more than Stella's killer. Hell, I owed Stella's killer a debt of gratitude, because whatever our burglar sought, he didn't find. "Me too, E.B."

She sat on the couch next to Don and swirled her drink like a cyclone. "They want to give a half million dollars for twenty five percent of your company, a company not worth a tenth of that."

That hurt. "Gee, thanks."

"Well, you have to admit, a half million dollars is a bit absurd." She tested her drink. "Every attorney I know doesn't buy anything unless they know there's something in it for them, and this office and business isn't it." She stood and walked to one of my filing cabinets. "Unless there's something in this office worth a hell of a lot more." She ran a hand over an old wooden filing cabinet recessed into the wall. "The killer interrupted him half way through his burglary."

Only half the room had been ransacked. "Obviously."

"And he started with these instead of your desk."

I shrugged. "And?"

"Are these cabinets yours?"

I shook my head. "They're built in."

"So, if you have to vacate, they stay?"

"Yep." Wow, I'm amazed I hadn't considered that. "There's something stashed away in this office." Maybe I did have a half million dollars sitting around the office.

"It would appear a lot more than that, but what's worth that much money?"

Chapter 42

Don's eyes lit up. From our conversation, he had input.

"Yes, Don?"

"When I had the bathroom built, they destroyed all my original cabinetry, even though I'd asked them to keep it."

"Are you suggesting they looked in your office as well?"

"Sort of looks that way."

"And why would a carpenter know to do that?"

"Hal was one of them."

So many things didn't make sense. "Why would he wait all these years to find whatever he's looking for?"

Don crossed his legs and had the air of someone in charge. "Has Hal talked to you recently about his father?"

"I don't communicate much with Hal. Ever since he took over from George, I've enjoyed our landlord tenant relationship. I don't complain and he leaves me alone."

"George is terminally ill."

About fucking time.

He was old as dirt. "And?"

"Do you remember Easter of O-five?"

George had begun the promenade ground work. The area consisted of a pile of torn up concrete. "The egg hunt?"

Don told Ebony the story. "George has an adult Easter egg hunt. He puts one-hundred dollar bills in all these eggs, but in one of the eggs, he puts the deed to his winter cabin."

I interrupted. "I don't remember that. How do you?"

"Because it's my cabin now."

"How come I never heard about that?"

Don shook his head. "The note inside the egg said, "Come to me for a secret. He said to keep it private, and I never told anyone I got the place from him."

"So do you think there are more proverbial eggs still around?"

"Maybe, and maybe he gave his kid a head start."

"What do you think he's giving away?"

"Don shrugged. "Could be anything, but clearly it has to be something he's owned for at least twenty years." He pointed at me. "Because if he planted something deep into the bowels of this room, he did it before you moved in."

George liked hard work. His kid had done his fair share, but he didn't have his dad's work ethic. It would fit George's personality to give away his fortune. I turned to Ebony. "Do you have a key to Stella's room?"

"No."

"Doesn't matter." I marched out of my office and over to her door, Don and Ebony following. They make office doors sturdy, but not sturdy enough for a man my size. I hit that thing with my shoulder and she snapped open. The three of us stood there, speechless by the sight of a room with the walls peeled away from the frame. "So much for forensics." I turned to Ebony. "E.B., you want to explain this?"

"I swear to God. When I left this room, three men in white suits were canvassing this room for blood evidence."

I exhaled. "Well, since that time, someone tore this place apart, slat by slat."

Don said. "Maybe they found what they were looking for."

"Doubtful." I grinned. "Those attorneys wouldn't be eager to still buy my company." I patted Don on the shoulder. "Let's go look at Henry's room."

"No need."

"Why?"

"He had his place remodeled the same year I did. They gutted his place." Don shook his head. "Don't you ever pay attention to your neighbors?"

"No Don, I don't. Personally, if you weren't such a needy shit, I probably wouldn't know your name." I reminded him. "High fences make great neighbors."

"Well, his place, I'm sure has been as canvassed as mine was."

I knew we could leave the four empty units alone. "That leaves just my office."

Ebony grabbed my arm. "Dick, this takes the investigation to a different place."

"Guess it moves Hal and his two siblings to the top of the list."

Ebony stared at Don. "Puts Don on that list too."

Don held a hand up. "Wait. Me? Why the hell am I now a suspect?"

She offered, "You knew Mr. Michaels gave stuff away."

Don's face flushed. "I'm guessing this is why these places were searched. I don't know anything."

I waved off Ebony. "Don is an obsequious turd, but he's my obsequious turd. He's not playing any angles." I squinted. "Are you, Don?"

"I should say not."

He stomped off, and we found him nursing his drink on the couch in my office. "Relax, that's her job. She checks people off the list and moves on."

"Still, it hurts to have my integrity compromised."

"Integrity? Good Lord, Don, you are a busybody. Paying attention to others behind their backs has less integrity than me ignoring them." I chided him. "Let me refresh that drink so you can build some more integrity."

"It's not funny, Dick."

Ebony didn't say a word. She glanced at me, and I leveled the moment with a whisper. "Don't worry, he'll be fine."

"Don, I'm sorry, sometimes I get in police mode and I didn't mean to imply you were a viable suspect."

"Apology accepted."

"Oh, I'm not apologizing. I'm just admitting you are low on the suspect list."

Don stood and turned to me. "I think my night is done. I need to get home to my wife." He turned to Ebony. "Officer Black, good night." He bowed and walked out of the room.

Ebony poured a drink. "Wow, he's a little sensitive."

"What do you expect? He's a foot doctor."

Ebony called after him. "Don, don't leave."

Of course, that's all the attention he needed. One smokin' hot chick calling him back and he returned and forgot the same woman had just insulted him.

Chapter 43

I barreled into those cabinets and used all my brute force to jar them loose. Not much of a carpenter I didn't have tools, and of all the fucking things Don could have had over there in his chamber of horrors office, not having a hammer made no sense. "Gawd damnit, Don, don't you have anything that can break these things apart?"

"Dick, I don't have those kind of tools."

"Fuck." I propped a foot up on the wall and reefed on the edge of the cabinet. It inched its way forward. Ebony joined in and together we tugged as the file gave way from the anchoring bolts. One by one, I separated all six cabinets from the wall.

Ebony pulled out each drawer and canvassed the inside of the cabinet. Each one had nothing.

She had a small utility flashlight. "Check to see if there is any yellowing where a paper may have been taped."

"Nothing."

"Well that was a waste." Not a damn thing in any of them.

Don offered, "Do you need help getting them back into place?"

"What?" My chest heaved from a workout. "I don't give a shit about these cabinets."

He shook his head. "It looks untidy."

I shrugged and went for my liquor. "Be my guest." I couldn't wait to see him try and scoot those cabinets back into place. Ebony moved to help him, and I caught her arm. "No, let him do it."

"Let me help him. Who knows it might work to our benefit if the person whose casing this room doesn't know we've looked."

"First off, you won't make it look natural, and they will clearly look like they've been disturbed."

"Just help." She turned and stood akimbo. "Okay?"

Fuck me.

She looked at me with those tits pointed right at me. I don't know if it was a case of colposinquanonia in me, or maybe looking at her lips caused a cheiloproclitic desire, but I couldn't resist her charm.

I caught a second wind and pushed off the desk. "Very well, but this better not burn off the good high I have."

She put her arm around my lower back and squeezed. "Don't worry, if it does, we'll just drink our way back."

That made sense.

We reorganized the cabinets, and Don turned from laborer into coxswain. I nearly bitch-slapped him when our last cabinet wouldn't seat and he offered from the couch a suggestion of putting more muscle into it. "Shut up, Don."

"Just saying, if you slid it back out and run it in, it'll push back far enough."

"Oh, just slide it back and run it in?"

"Yeah."

You want to show me?" That ended the conversation.

The sweat running off Ebony's chest soaked her top and for as transparent as her tee shirt had been, it left nothing for the imagination after our work. "E.B. you better hope no one else shows up." I undressed her with my fixed slobbering stare.

"Sorry, I guess with the liquor and the work, I sort of sweated a little."

"A little?"

She looked down. "Well, clearly you can see no hair is growing."

As much as I really wanted to keep staring, I suggested she grab one of Don's scrubs from his office.

"Don, can I?"

Don sat mesmerized.

"Don!" I snapped my fingers.

"Oh, yeah, go ahead." He stood, "Here, let me help you."

Idiot.

He followed her like a puppy. "Hey, we're done, so if you want to go home, you can."

He turned. "Are you sure?"

"Yeah, just get her a new top and you can go."

"Are you sure?" Son of a bitch begged in his question.

"Yes, Don."

He nodded and led Ebony to his office. I poured a drink and nursed it while I waited.

Ebony returned with a pea green top that floated on her. I should have kept my yap shut.

"You don't like it?" She twirled and held her arms out.

"Not particularly."

"You like this better?" She pulled it off and still had her wet tee shirt on.

"What the?"

"Dick, the look on your face every time you ogle my breasts is worth a damp shirt. Besides, I'm showered and perfumed, so I don't stink."

What the hell was she doing? I thought she was supposed to be my protection, not my tease. My dick begged like a dog in heat.

"So did you make me a drink too?"

I poured a whiskey coke, and she snagged a piece of limp pizza. "So here's how this nights going down. You have that nice big chair, and I have this couch. Sorry, but the blanket is staying with me. So we might as well drink awhile so you don't have to be too uncomfortable in that chair."

"E.B., it won't be the first time I've slept in this chair. You just better be drunk enough to not care about my snoring."

"I plan on passing out, don't worry about me."

"Get comfortable then."

Chapter 44

"How come you never remarried?" She held her cup like a hot chocolate by the fire, pressed close to her lips as she questioned my private life.

"I did such a splendid job the first time."

"Well, sounds like it had more to do with who you picked than how you treated her."

I agreed. "Yeah, that too, but let's face it, besides not picking women very well, I'm not the most attentive guy."

She tilted her head and stared at me. "I don't see that. I see a man who is rather short with arrogant people yet rather giving."

What the fuck? Is she psycho analyzing me?

"You haven't been around me long enough."

She winked. "I like what I see."

Oh wow, erection city.

"Don't let that alcohol get the best of you."

She changed the subject. "Has it dawned on you that somewhere in this room is something worth killing for?" She steered me away from my gaze.

"Of course."

"You know what it is?"

"I don't know, let me think about it. I have some ideas."

She stood, walked over to my chair and sat on my lap. "Care to tell me what you think it is?" She put her arm around my neck, and those luscious lips met mine with a soft passionate embrace.

I did a quick inventory to make sure I hadn't slipped into dream mode. "Don't you want to know?" For all my bravado, I never much cared to force myself on anyone. She must have sensed that, because she didn't appear to plan on letting me say no.

She slid a leg over my lap and faced me, straddling my waist like a motorcycle. She took the base of her tee shirt and twisted it up and over her chest and tossed it to the floor. "Not really." Her arms wrapped around my neck, and for the next two minutes she found every inch of my face. "Does that feel good?" She whispered as she wet my ear.

Let this not be alcohol related, please.

Waking up next to a cop I'd just fucked and her patting her pussy to see it had cum on it, and then shooting me would not make my day. "Are you okay?"

She put her hands on my shoulders and leaned back, her tits as firm as drum skins, dark areolas and eraser sized nipples. "Do you think this is a drunken come on?"

"Is it?"

"Would it matter if it was?"

I wanted to bounce this cute thing up and down and hear her squeal like a homecoming queen, I really did, but not if she wouldn't remember, and definitely not if she would regret it. "Yeah, it would matter."

She tilted her head. "Why?"

"Because I like you. I could hang with you—" I shrugged. "A long, long time."

She smiled, and an angelic recognition crossed her face. "You are a beautiful man."

"Let's not get carried away. You must be drunk."

"If I am, I suspect you will fuck the drunk right out of me."

I sat up, she barely weighed a buck ten, stood and she wrapped her legs around me. I carried her to the couch and before I laid her down, something caught my eye; something caught my eye and my memory. "Shit."

Ebony clung to me. "What?"

"E.B., I may or may not know what they are after, but I will bet money I know where it is."

She twisted her head to catch what I had my gaze fixed on. "Behind the mirror?"

"George replaced that mirror himself about ten years ago. Didn't need it but he did it anyway. Bastard screwed that thing in like he worried an earthquake would bring it down." I put Ebony down and she retrieved her tee shirt.

"I'll resume our other conversation later." She moved to the mirror above the cabinets and counted the screws. "Good Lord, how many screws are in it?" She counted off thirty. "That many screws for a mirror the size of manhole cover?" She turned to me. "You have a screwdriver?"

"Phillips or standard?"

"Phillips."

Like it mattered. "No."

We could hear Don locking up, and Ebony hurried to the door. She blurted, "Don, do you have a screwdriver?"

I came up behind Ebony as Don nodded. "Still hunting I see."

"Something like that." I needed him to hurry. "Do you?"

"Can I help?"

"You can help by not making your wife upset."

He turned to Ebony. "Are you sure you couldn't use my help?"

"We're okay, Don. We just want to make sure that we haven't overlooked anything."

Don reversed course and returned with an electric drill and a set of drivers.

"Wow, Dr. Coleman, you're a prepared man." There she went again, flattering Don. Shit, we would never get rid of him at this rate.

As we turned, Don started to follow but Ebony stopped him. "Don, go home to your lovely wife. Besides, I don't want to have to protect you too."

Don's face paled. "Seriously, do you expect trouble?"

Ebony waved him on to the elevator. "You never know." She encouraged him to leave, and we scanned the hallway before locking the door behind us.

I knew he'd hidden something behind that mirror, and I emptied the screws like a pit crew at a raceway. When the mirror lifted away from the wall—nothing.

Not a fucking thing.

"What? I was so sure something would be here."

Ebony rubbed my back. "If it's any consolation, you're welcome to come lay on the couch with me."

Oops, erection.

Chapter 45

"Are you going to put it back up?" Ebony handed me the drill.

"Fuck it." I put the mirror on top of the cabinet and plopped down onto the couch. When I turned back to Ebony, Gawd damned if she didn't have her top off and her pants down to a pair of red bikini lace panties.

"Hello." I observed. "I thought you said you weren't wearing any underwear."

"I lied." She climbed back onto my lap. "Now where were we?"

I couldn't help but notice she worked out. Instead of a flat stomach, she had six oblique muscles that tightened her mid section. I scooted her closer so a few scant pieces of material separated her crotch and my dick. She ground herself into my waist, grabbed my hair on both sides of my temples, and shoved my head back so she could plant her tongue into my mouth, only she banged my head against the cabinet and the mirror tumbled down on top of my scalp. I could hear the glass crack and Ebony froze.

"What? Am I bleeding?" I remained still to keep from cutting myself further.

"No, you aren't bleeding."

"What then?"

"It wasn't behind the mirror." She reached with both hands and lifted the mirror off my head. A single crack across the center left a gap. "It's inside the mirror."

In between the crack I could make out a document. "Seven years bad luck."

Ebony reminded me, "Broke on your head, not mine." She slid off me. "I guess this means a time-out again?"

As she redressed, I snapped the mirror like an egg and separated the glass from the backing. "E.B., these are worth killing someone for."

She fitted the tee shirt over her shoulders. "Is anything worth killing someone for?"

"If money's a motive, then these are worth it."

"What are those, bank notes?"

"Deeds."

She came up alongside me and sat. "To?"

Inside the mirror, George had stuffed deeds for his home, his private plane, yacht, and about twenty pieces of property, including the buildings and garage of the promenade. "I think everything he owns."

She riffled the paper. "How many are there?"

George had amassed a fair chunk of land over the years. From the South Bay all the way to Pasadena, it appeared he held a thousand acres of developed property. "I'm guessing close to a billion dollars."

"Get out of town," Ebony lit up like a Christmas tree. "What does this mean to you?"

"Knowing George and his hide-and-seek games, I'd say it means. 'Finders keepers, losers weepers.'"

I walked to my desk and picked up Dee's manuscript. I slipped the deeds between the sheets, put them back in her manila envelope and placed it on the pile of debris manuscripts.

"What are you doing?"

"If we are ambushed, there's one place they'll never look."

"Dick, if we are ambushed, we are as good as dead for that kind of property."

"Officer Black, I have much more faith in your detail abilities than that."

She stood akimbo, staring at the pile. "What makes you think it's safe with me knowing it's there?"

"I don't, but at some point I have to trust someone or be paranoid for every person who comes through that door."

The words hadn't spent their noise when someone knocked.

Ebony pursed her lips and held a finger up. She tiptoed to the door and listened. I froze. My weight would set off creaks in that old building.

A second knock followed by, "Come on guys, let me in."

Fucking Don.

I could pretty much forget Ebony's vagina. "What do you want, Don?"

"My car won't start."

I motioned to let him in.

Ebony unlocked the door, and Don bounced in. "So did you find anything?"

I developed suspicion. "Why do you want to know?"

"Just asking, Jeez, what a crank pot." He came in as though he lived with me, tossed his coat on the couch and slapped his hands together. "Anything I can do to help?"

I hadn't moved, just rotated my view as he stumbled around the room. "What's wrong with your car?"

"I don't know, it goes ur ur ur, but doesn't start up."

What a simpleton.

"That's turning over, and it won't fire." I tried to troubleshoot. "Are you out of gas?"

"Oh, gosh no, I never let it fall below half."

Must be nice to not be down to one's last fucking nickel half the time.

"Did you pop the hood to see if your plugs were in place?" Stupid question, anyone who says, 'ur, ur,' hasn't a clue what plugs are, not to mention, he drove around in a brand new car with a smog cover. You can't get to the plugs. "Never mind."

"Can I hang out here?"

"Why don't you call your wife and have her come get you."

"Come on, Dick. Let me hang out with you guys. Let me drink those brain thingies with you."

Ebony moved around us and went to the desk, my temporary bar table. She poured Baileys, peach schnapps, and grenadine, before she picked it up, I motioned to the whiskey. She chastised me with a scowl but complied, pouring a good shot in with it. We'd see how long he'd hang with us, and if he had any ulterior motive, I'd get him singing in no time.

Ebony played good hostess, I played bad hostess. I sneered and leaned against the desk while my foot doctor friend questioned, "This one tastes different."

I admitted, "It's an Irishman's brain."

"What's that mean?"

"Nothing, just enjoy it."

He pounded that bitch like a college kid out on his twenty-first birthday.

Ebony made him a second, and poured whiskeys for me and her. She parked herself in front of me and leaned hard against me. With one hand, she raised her drink in salute to Don, and with the other, she reached behind her and grabbed my wiener. She grabbed my wiener and made it pay attention. We downed our drinks and she tilted her head back and looked up at me. She reached up, grabbed the back of my head and forced me down to kiss her.

Don blurted, "Holy cow, are you two kissing?"

Ebony had shot her entire drink back into mouth. "No, I was just force feeding him."

I winked. "You want to try?"

Don smiled. "Yeah."

I said, "Ebony, give me a shot to stick in my mouth."

Don squirmed. "No! Never mind."

"Come on, Don. I'll give you a shot."

"No, no, no."

Ebony broke in. "If I gave you the shot would you take it?"

Don nodded.

"And your wife wouldn't get jealous?"

"If we didn't tell her, she would have no reason to be jealous."

Ebony turned. "Don is on his way to stitches, Dick." She winked and spun back around to Don "There is a rule to this game."

"What's that?"

"Whatever shot I give you, you have to give me. However, you do five in a row; then you give me five in a row."

Don had no problem with that. I sort of did, but he didn't. I interrupted, "Wait—"

Ebony patted my crotch. "Just you relax." She grabbed the whiskey and sat next to Don. She tilted the bottle to her lips and took in six ounces if she took a drop. She leaned over to Don, and like one balloon to another, her cheeks deflated and his expanded. Don's eyes teared up, and Ebony put her hand over Don's mouth to keep him from spitting. "Swallow it, honey."

Pipsqueak did it, but I had to rush a glass of coke to him.

He wiped his mouth and coughed. "Four more, right?"

That girl knew a few tricks. "Ready?"

Before Don could catch his breath, she shot another wad of whiskey into his mouth. Again, she held him from spitting it up. "You don't want to soil your couch, Don."

I handed him another coke. Ebony held a hand up, one more and we could wait a few minutes before he went down.

After the third mega-shot went in, Ebony suggested he wait a few minutes for the fourth one. Don had no problems with that. A few minutes pushed into ten and down went Don.

"Check his coat for his keys."

Ebony followed me over to Don's office; we deposited him on his couch and covered him up with a blanket—one that matched his décor. He'd be proud of me for that. We locked him in and retreated back to my office.

Ebony worried, "I hope he'll be okay over there."

"I just hope I'll be okay over here."

"Oh, Dick," she closed the door behind us and locked it, "you are going to be just fine."

Chapter 46

The night quieted, the promenade below had shut down to street sweepers and late night restaurants. The fountain stilled and amber lights cast shadows of nothing. Ebony turned the light off and a yellow glow cut through the slats like zebra impressions against our skin. She pushed me toward the couch until I buckled and sat on a cushion. The light danced off her, and I could make out breasts as she removed her top. She slipped off her sandals, unsnapped her pants, and they fell to the floor. She stepped out of them and kneeled before me.

"You're not drunk, right?"

"Shut up, Dick." She worked my belt and popped each button of my trousers. I lifted my legs and she slid off my pants. "A boxer man."

"Yeah, well, with a few extra pounds, briefs don't help my ego." My cock had once again perked up. That poor thing must have worried something fierce over the last three hours of being teased to death.

Ebony tugged at my boxers, and I lifted my butt as she worked them down my thighs. When she'd freed me, she worked her way up my legs until she found my penis. "Holy shit."

"What?"

She stood and scrambled for the light. From across the room she had this look of horror on her face. "My God, you weren't kidding."

"You mean this?" I fumbled with my joy stick. "I'm not even that hard yet."

"Muffin must be hollow inside." Ebony's expression bordered on frightened.

"Well, no one's ever been killed by it."

"I hope I'm not the first." She caught the edge of her panties and rolled them off her waist, and a little landing strip of pubic hair came into view.

"Aren't you going to turn the lights off?"

"No, I'm both amazed and worried. I think I should have the lights on." She walked up to the couch and straddled me.

"Don't you want foreplay?"

"Dick, I'm so wet looking at that right now, I could crawl on the floor and leave a trail like a slug." She grabbed my penis and mounted me. A third of the way down, she stopped and shivered. "Oh, this is going to hurt so good."

I'd learned years before not to grab my women and shove them down. It often stopped sex for the evening. I held still as she went down a few more inches.

"Am I there yet?"

I peered past her tits, past that tight stomach and saw lots of daylight between us; she was stuck like a popsicle. "Nope, you have quite a ways to go." I suspected this was going to be a night of screaming.

She put her hands on my shoulders to steady her descent, her eyes rolled somewhere behind her eyelids and she shrieked. "I don't know whether to love you or hate you." She continued, and to my amazement, made it to where we ground hip to hip. She didn't pull away, instead just twisted me inside her. Her eyes had closed and her upper lip beaded with sweat. She drew herself closer and her nipples turned solid as they danced over my chest. She chirped in my ear, a soft, high, tearful whimper. She passed between "Holy mother of God," and straight up screaming. I let her fit with me until she wanted something more.

"Lay me on my back."

I rolled her off and stayed inside as I put her down. I started to lift her leg but she stopped me.

"I can't take you that deep."

"I guess anal's out of the question?"

Her eyes popped open. "You aren't serious."

"No, just kidding."

Although if she says absolutely I will give it the old college try.

I leaned in and kissed her. I slowly pushed in and pulled out. Each drive forward, she let out a peep of pain. "Are you sure you want to do this?"

She reached up to my cheeks and held them in her hands. "I'm in heaven, don't stop."

I fucked her for an hour until exhaustion blurted out, "I've come so many times I can't come anymore, and the truth is I'm pretty sure you've torn me up." She reached between her legs and held onto me as I slid out. "Wait."

"What?"

"You are hard as a rock."

"So."

"Go back in." She reached up and dug her nails into my back. "Stroke, big boy."

I pumped, and she locked onto my lips and darted her tongue against mine. She knew what to do, and two minutes in, I'd exploded.

"Don't pull out; just roll me on top of you."

I changed position and she fell asleep on my chest, still stuck to me like an umbilical cord.

I pulled the blanket down and wrapped it over us. She didn't move, worn out, our warm sweat sliding between us.

I didn't mind the lights, she looked golden and beautiful. "Goodnight E.B."

She found my hand and locked her fingers into mine.

Chapter 47

Fucking taste in my mouth. At least it isn't the grit of pussy hair.

I focused on the ceiling and realized Ebony wasn't on my chest. I didn't move—a static of disturbance swirled around me. Something, or someone, had been there. I could sense it. "E.B.?" Nothing. I sat up and scanned the room. My clothes were gone, so was Dee's manila envelope.

Fuck me, just like the scent of pussy to distract me.

Could I be that stupid? Let's see, attractive younger woman on a cop's salary. Yep, pretty much summed it up, I was a retard. On my desk sat Ebony's flak jacket and my shirt, nothing else. I stuck my naked rump into my leather comfy, nothing like the feel of flesh on leather to wake me up.

That was some expensive pussy.

Some people are meant to have good luck, while others, if they didn't have bad luck wouldn't have any at all. I picked up the jacket, and realized how petite Ebony's was. I released the straps as far as they could go and tried it on. "Fucking uncomfortable." I flexed my pecs and couldn't imagine walking around in that piece of shit. I grabbed my shirt and put it on, viewed myself to see how bulky I looked. If I didn't seem overweight before, I certainly did with that jacket on.

My door flew open and in walked Don. "You should lock your door."

"No shit. Welcome to the biggest moron's office in the world."

"What?"

"I appear to have been fleeced," I stood and exposed that I had no clothes below my shirt, "by a cop no less."

"Oh, oh no." Don tried to turn away, but he kept staring at me. "Is that really your male sexual organ?"

"It's called a dick, Don."

"Do you have a condition?" He walked toward me, pulled out a latex glove, intent on inspecting it.

When he reached toward my wiener, I stopped him. "What are you doing?"

"That looks ungodly swollen."

I placed it in my hand and twisted to the right and left. "Nope, it's actually behaving well right now."

"Wait, it gets bigger?"

"Lots bigger."

Don sat on the edge of my desk. "I don't believe it. Make it get bigger."

"I'm not going to make it get bigger." I scowled. "Bend over and I'll stick it in you."

"You're disgusting, Dick."

I turned to my issues. "Damn it. Don, I found it last night, and now it's all gone."

"What did you find?"

"Everything. George had deeds for every God damned item he owned and stuffed it in a mirror in this office."

"Oh." Don's dejected expression moped how George didn't love him enough to leave it in his room.

"You'd be dead right now if it'd been in your room, so consider yourself lucky."

"You want me to go get you some pants?"

"What do you have, hospital scrubs?"

"Yep."

I sat back in my chair. "Yeah, gonna need something before Jim, Jim Hunter and Muffin arrive." Funny, but that dick wad attorney was going to get his. He'd pay a half million for nothing but this office. Sadly, my skanky ex would make bank.

Don hadn't crossed the hall when he stepped back in, backwards with his hands raised. Walking him in, a portly fat-ass detective.

"But of course, L.A.'s finest." Let me guess, she couldn't finish the job, and you are here to clean it up."

Littleton closed the door behind him and motioned for Don to find a seat on the couch. "What the hell are you talking about?"

He doesn't know.

I weighed my options. His knowing didn't help my cause. "I lost my detail and assumed you were here to help me."

"Funny, Mr. Dillard." Littleton kept his pistol trained on me as he checked the restroom. He returned. "Where is Black?"

"I sent her home. The day's done, I assumed I was safe." I checked my clock. "It's 5:30, didn't think I had to worry."

He chewed on a toothpick. "You thought wrong."

"Yeah, so have you been behind all the killing around here?"

"Nope, but I'm going to be behind these two."

Don toggled his concern between the detective and me. "Wait, what did I do?"

I gave him a nod. "Don, you are in the wrong place at the wrong time."

"So, look, the way I see it, I have about two hours to tear this place apart. We can do it the easy way, which I realize won't help you, but it'll make my life a lot easier, or we can do it the hard way where I do the search on my own."

Don started to say something, but I shut him up. Our only leverage was Littleton not knowing those deeds came and went. If he knew the deeds weren't here, he had no use for us. Don shook like a wet poodle.

"Tell me, Littleton, who do you think killed Stella?"

"I don't know, and I don't care. What I do know is at this end of this day, you will have killed her, and that little fuck foot doctor is your accomplice, and if I hadn't been trained as a marksman, I would have been ambushed. Thankfully, I got the upper hand and shot the two perps. And tomorrow, I'll retire and live out my days on a yacht." He waved his gun. "Stand up."

I stood, and he froze. "Holy Shit." He stepped closer, "Gawd Damn."

"You want to touch it?"

He shook his head. "I have a new found respect for your ex-wife. I can't believe you didn't kill her with that."

"If I could have I would have, trust me."

Littleton smiled. "Tell me about it. Best thing about sailing off into the sunset will be leaving my beast I have at home."

"You might want to do something with her too, because you know she'll get half of everything."

"I'll keep that in mind." He started to say something but my wiener must have mesmerized him. "You are the reason why guys like me have complexes."

"If it makes you feel any better, it's gotten me in more trouble than it's worth."

"Really?"

I shook my head. "No, that's a lie, it's great, and I love having it."

"Fuck you, Dillard." He raised the gun, but the door swung open.

"Detective Littleton?"

Littleton spun around and had a faceoff with Hal. Hal had a gun trained on him, and Littleton did likewise.

"Are you considering taking what's mine?"

"Hey, Mexican standoff." I crossed me arms.

Hal came into the room and closed the door. He made reference to me. "What the hell happen to you?"

"Why?"

"Did this jack off pistol whip your dick?" He and Littleton kept their weapons trained on each other as Hal stepped closer. "Damn, that's swollen."

Littleton agreed. "I know, right?"

"It's not swollen, hell, it's still sleeping."

"Wow, no wonder my dad thought you were a man's man." Hal turned to Littleton. "Are you seriously going to rob me of my inheritance?"

"The way I see it, your father doesn't think much of you, because he has left this for anyone who finds it, and a numbnut kid who tells his attorney why he needs this room isn't fit to have it." He glared at Hal. "How the fuck do you think I knew about it?"

As much as I wanted those two idiots to start firing, we had more company. Someone tapped hard on the glass. "Damn it," I hollered over my captor, "Don't break my glass!"

The door opened and my day couldn't get any better.

Chapter 48

In walked a beat up Jim Hunter and his smoking hot sister, Jamie. Littleton pulled out a second gun. I suspected the one he planned to plant on me before this fiasco of an idea went south.

"Littleton, this is turning really bad." I hadn't moved, just a spectator in his comedy of errors.

"Then we'll need to even the playing field." Without any fanfare, he fired a single shot into Hal's forehead. Jim and Jamie froze, Don cried like a girl who'd lost her virginity the hard way, and Hal crumpled. No words, no music, just a pile on my floor.

When the smoke cleared, Jim noticed me. "I see Littleton beat you too?"

"Huh?"

He motioned to my wiener. "Looks like he beat that thing silly."

Jamie fixed on it, and didn't seem to care that Littleton had a gun on her. She approached. "Shut up, Jimmy. That's a thing of beauty."

I didn't know I could achieve an erection in the face of life threatening danger, but that little spinner had me seeking attention.

Littleton shouted. "Stop that. I don't want to see that thing stand up."

I sat, and Jamie motioned if she had permission to sit on my lap.

Littleton waved her on. "If it'll hide that thing, go for it."

I made her comfortable on my lap. "Are you in this with your brother?"

She shook her head. "I just came along because he said the officer beat him up, and he was coming to warn you."

"Is that true, Jim?"

"Scout's honor." He stayed put, his fear held him against the wall. "Hal told me what he had and offered me a cool million. I might be a lot of things, but a killer isn't one of them."

"Did Hal kill Stella?"

"No."

"Are you sure?"

"Pretty sure."

I swiveled toward Littleton, Jamie grinding on my wiener like a pogo stick. "Are you even the least bit curious about this case?"

"I told you before, as far as I'm concerned, you and the foot doctor did it."

"Be that as it may, you are now in the midst of a spree killing if you kill us all."

"I'm not killing you all. Hal was killed with your gun." He waved the plant in my face. "Just as the brother and sister were."

Jim's face tightened as the words left Littleton's lips, but Jamie piped up. "Eww, such violence, Detective Littleton.

"Unless you want to come with me, I guess violence will be your demise."

"You got a dingaling like this guy," she patted my shoulder, "and I'll consider it."

"Honey, I don't think anyone has something like that."

She rubbed my head and whispered, "Now I know why you don't give a shit about much in life. You are the cock of the walk." While she mesmerized Littleton with her conversation, she used a little prestidigitation to shove a handgun into my lap. She squeezed my wiener on the way out. "Any other day and I would make that my own personal slurpy."

Somehow having her gnawing on my flesh made for pleasant thoughts. "Let's get out of this mess first."

Littleton had had enough. "You know, Dillard, you of all people scare me the most. The woman's right, you don't seem to give a shit about anything, and for that, I need to eliminate you. He lifted his gun and before I could get a grip on the weapon in my lap, the door swung open and the cackle of Muffin's voice sent shivers down my spine.

"Not so fast."

Another Mexican standoff as Charles and Littleton squared off. Muffin still expected that sorry sad sack to mind her coat. "Here, Charles." He kept one gun on Littleton and worked as a coat boy with the other.

Muffin McCready walked in without fear of reproach. "If anyone is killing Dick, it'll be me." I moved Jamie off my lap and stood.

When Muffin saw me in the buff, she insisted I sit back down, but the damage was done. Poor Charles looked like I'd mortally wounded him. "Muffin, you never told me about that?" He stepped closer to his wife. "That explains a lot of things."

I interrupted, "She ever ask if you were in yet?"

"How did you know?"

"Don't feel bad Charles, she said the same thing to me."

"Bullshit. I never said anything. I was too busy having my lady cage torn open." She gave me the stink eye.

"Lady cage? That's a fucking Venus fly trap."

"You piece of shit."

"Skank."

"Bastard."

"Bitch."

"Asshole."

Littleton pointed his second gun at Muffin. "The two of you shut the fuck up."

Speechless.

Muffin was speechless, and to think all it took was a revolver to her face.

I could see Littleton's agitation toward my ex. His finger twitched on that trigger. "Muffin, just back up and take a position alongside your husband, Okay?"

Reality had sunk in, and she did as I told her.

First fucking time in her life.

Littleton stretched his arm out in Charles' direction. "I'm done. Put the gun down, Nimrod." He motioned to Muffin. "Tell him to put down the gun, or I make sure you are the first person dead?"

Muffin pointed to Hal. "Second."

"I really want to kill you, so say another word besides, 'honey, put down the gun,' and I will do it with pleasure."

Not that I wanted Muffin dead, or perhaps dead would be fantastic, but putting the gun down didn't strike me as a bright move; however, like the drone he'd become, Charles did as Muffin told him and held one hand up and leaned forward with his gun, placing it on the ground.

Idiot.

"Now, slide it over to me."

All the while, Jamie nudged me to take the hand gun nestled next to my balls and do battle.

Bystanders in all this, the two most educated saps in the room were petrified. Dr. Coleman had his hands in his lap like a Sunday-school teacher, and Jim, Jim Hunter played mannequin against the wall.

"Now, I need all of you right here, on your knees."

What a tool.

He'd already told Don and me how he planned on killing everyone. All six of us looked at him like he was a fucking moron. "Seriously?"

"You have an issue with that, Dillard?"

I tucked the handgun into the cushion and stood. It might not have looked macho, standing in a faceoff with my dong dragging like an anchor, but I leaned over my desk with my knuckles holding me up. I reminded detective Dickhead, "Why the fuck would we line up when you said you were shooting us?"

"Because, of all people, I would think you would appreciate taking it like a man."

I tilted my head. "You haven't thought this out, have you? You might get away with your bullshit story with a hole in those four heads, but Don and I sort of have to be shot face to face."

"Fine I'll shoot you right now."

"Fuck you, Tubby."

Chapter 49

Don continued to cry; Muffin had a smile. I think seeing my cock made her fall in love with me all over again. The clock chimed six o'clock. The boards creaked and someone came down the hallway, check that, several people came down the hallway. I circled my desk. They stopped at my door. Through the opaque glass, I could see a crowd. All of us turned—waiting. We were dormice, and a faint, "one, two, three," preceded the door flying open. Four young men carrying bats rushed in. Leading the charge was my young adversary; two black eyes, a nasty cut across his nose, and one ear bandaged. They stopped when they met the end of Littleton's barrel.

"You boys lost?"

Their bats dropped and their hands shot up.

With cotton in his nose, and a nasally congestion, the kid said, "Holy Shit." His hands reached skyward, but he used a finger to point at me. "Why are you naked, why is your dick the biggest thing I've ever seen, and why is there a dead man on the floor?" He motioned toward Littleton. "And why does that man have a gun on us?"

"Well, I'm naked because someone took my clothes, my cock is big because I'm a man and you're not; the man of the floor was shot by this man who has a gun on all of us."

"Well, if that's what it takes to be a man, I haven't met too many men."

Littleton didn't have the sense to close the door, so when the café clerk showed up on their heels, the detective waved him in. "Close that door behind you."

"What's going on here?"

Littleton became the headmaster of a classroom. "Who are you?"

"I work downstairs at the coffee shop." He had a stoned expression and must have thought it strange Don and the four young men had their hands up.

"What do you want?"

"I'm here to deliver some poetry to Mr. Dillard." He caught a glimpse of me and said, "Holy Shit."

Littleton turned to me. "You publish poetry?"

Fuck no.

"Sometimes, if it's exceptional."

Littleton's eyes lit up. "I write poetry."

I knew there was a reason, besides being a douche bag greedy Down syndrome cop, why I didn't like him. "You want me to look at it?"

"Damn it, I wish I'd known yesterday, I would have brought it up."

The café kid stepped forward. "Can I give this to Mr. Dillard?"

Littleton nodded. "Yeah, go ahead."

He stepped over Hal. "A publisher with a penis that big, I'm doing a poem about it at the next poetry slam."

"Okay Elizabeth Browning, you might want to think about the present situation before you start canonizing me."

He turned to Littleton, then to the seven across the room. "Uh oh. This isn't good, is it?"

I sighed. "You are a regular Robert Frost."

Littleton directed traffic. "You and the pretty blonde, over there with the other seven."

I grabbed Jamie and planted a kiss on her lips.

Her knees buckled and she shut her eyes. She reached down and gave my dick a yank. "Thank you."

I released her and winked at her brother who, to his credit, kept his composure and remained silent. I let her go and stood in front of Littleton, arms akimbo like Superman. "You have enough bullets in that gun?"

"Plenty."

Through the mail slot an envelope tumbled in, and someone knocked on the door. I stepped around my desk and walked toward it.

Littleton insisted I stop. "Where are you going?"

I saw the name Dee. "Fuck you, this is way more important than those deeds, you colostomy bag. This is my legacy."

I swung the door open, and honestly, I hadn't thought that one through. I hadn't seen this woman in twenty years and having my dick as my calling card wasn't how I envisioned our reunion. With her daughter, my daughter, standing beside her, it dawned on me how terribly wrong that looked.

She scanned me from top to bottom. "Yeah, that's the Dick I remember."

"Holy Shit, Mother. That was inside you?"

"That's in your genes, sweetheart."

I tried to push the two of them away, but Richelle ducked under my arm, and her mother followed suit.

Littleton shrieked, fit to be tied. "Jesus, where are all you people coming from at this time of the fucking morning?" He kept his gun trained on me as he made his way to the door. "That's it! No more people." He locked it. "Now, all of you line up against that wall."

I had a daughter in the room; things had changed. "Littleton, let these people go."

"I don't think you get it. I'm going to find those deeds."

"I already did."

He stuffed the barrel against my chest. "Then I would suggest you give them up."

"I can't."

He percolated, a slow boil seething his posture. "Why the fuck not?"

Muffin chimed in. "Yeah, why not, Dick?"

"Your subordinate took them."

Muffin cackled. "Priceless. I bet that's why you're naked. Did she fuck the documents out of you, Dick?"

God, I hated her. "Shoot her first, please."

Littleton nodded. "I know, right."

"Oh Muffin, by the way, I swept my hand toward Dee. "I'd like you to meet someone I fucked while I was married to you, and it produced that lovely young lady with her. Muffin, Dee. Dee, Muffin. The young lady is my daughter, Richelle."

Muffin insisted. "Shoot him, now."

Chapter 50

"Detective Littleton," I decided to give reason one more shot. He seemed to have jettisoned that part of his plan between 'I've got a plan' and 'haven't thought it through.' "Right now you may have killed the mastermind of the death of Stella. You aren't in too deep."

Littleton vacillated. I could hear the squeak in his ass. "I'm listening."

"Stella's death wasn't a coincidence. Her room and mine were the only two that hadn't been thoroughly gutted." I worked him. "When you did your forensics, had her room been ransacked?"

"Her bathroom had."

"Did your forensic team tear out the walls afterward?"

"No." He kept his gun focused on me. "I show up after hours the next day and Hal and this jackass," he pointed to Jim, "are stripping paneling, taking out the cabinets, lifting carpet."

"What did Hal say they were doing?"

"Crazy fucker said he was preparing it for new tenancy." His head bounced with understanding, "but I knew that little weasel attorney knew more, so I tailed him. He kept trying to call someone who I am sure has something to do with all of this, but I don't know who yet."

I offered. "About him, I think he's in the elevator motor room."

Littleton glared at Jim. "Anyway, when I couldn't get answers, I beat it out of him, and the rest is why we are standing here right now."

I faced Jim. "Your client either swore you to secrecy, or he hid something from you. Who else knew?"

Jim shrugged. "I don't know."

Jamie fired up. "Tell him, Jimmy."

His face turned sullen. "Shut up, Sis."

"No! Tell them."

I waved her off. "He doesn't have to. I know." I turned back to the detective. "Do you seriously believe that kid would be the attorney Hal would turn to for a billion dollar mystery? You might think you have this all figured out, that you're going to kill all these people and then pin it on Don and me, but you make it half way out of the bay with George's yacht, and I can pretty much promise you that the father and granddad of those two," I smiled at Jamie, "will hunt you down and hang you up to dry." I stood over Littleton, peering down at his fat face. "That kid hasn't done anything without his dad knowing."

He stepped back and reminded me he held the gun. "I don't give a shit. I've been a fucking underpaid detective for twenty years. I've cleaned floors with the likes of those pieces of shit attorneys, and I'll clean the ocean floor with them if they come after me."

There was no reasoning with that clown. "You will be fish bait."

"I'll be fish bait long after they bury you." He had a hatred for me that went well beyond my much bigger dick.

"When is enough enough?"

"When I get what's coming to me."

The fat kid in the group of four interrupted us. "Excuse me, but I have to pee. Can I use the rest room?"

Littleton held his two guns up. "Which one of these guns asked you to speak?"

"I really have to go."

"Then pee your pants."

I took another angle. "Has it dawned on you that you have thirteen people…" I discounted Hal, "twelve people here, and you haven't asked for one cell phone?"

"Shit." He shoved a gun my direction. "Give me yours."

I pointed out that my dick swung loosely in the breeze. "Do I look like I have one on me?"

"Good point." He turned to Muffin and Charles. "You two?"

Muffin shrugged. "My battery's dead, and I don't let Charles have a phone."

I intervened. "Why the fuck not?"

"He's with me, Dick. I set the rules."

Littleton sighed. "She really is a bitch."

The four boys didn't have a cell phone between them, Dee left hers in the car, Don left his in his office. The attorneys decided having something that could bounce off a tower wouldn't be wise. That left my daughter. Littleton backed her up. "You look guilty of something."

"You want this?" Richelle produced a phone.

Littleton snatched it and pulled something up. "You little bitch. You fucking called the cops." He raised his gun and Dee pleaded.

"Please don't hurt her."

"Littleton, you shoot her, and I swear you won't turn fast enough to keep me from breaking your neck."

He held the guns like Jesus hanging on the cross, one spread wide at me and the other wide at Richelle.

"Just relax. You're a cop." I turned to the rest of the room. "And the rest of you, one person has a working phone? Seriously? What year is this?"

Littleton pulled a phone from his pocket. "Two have a phone." He dialed up a number and in a short sentence took control of the disturbance at the promenade. He hung up. "Looks like no one's coming. I've got things covered."

Only thing was, he didn't have things covered. The room creaked from heavy steps in the hall. Everyone hesitated, taking in what felt like a cow walking.

"What the hell is that?"

Littleton stepped behind me and put the gun in my back. "No offense, but you're my shield."

"Thanks."

Whoever it was, their image reached over my glass door frame. "I think we're about to meet a whole lot of trouble."

Chapter 51

The door handle jiggled.

Littleton wetted my ear. "Damn glad I locked that."

One knock, one fucking knock, and twenty years of beauty evaporates.

My glass window shattered when whomever was on the other side banged on the door. "Fucking retard."

Fucking giant retard.

"Can I help you?" It didn't take Einstein to know this was our mysterious giant. In front of me, reaching in to unlock the door, stood the ugliest six ten woman I'd ever seen. Built like a freight train, she wiped a lock of blonde hair from her face. "Mr. Dillard, I'm here to discuss my manuscript."

"Mrs. Howard?"

Don came alive. "Mrs. Howard? That's Howard Timmons, Stella's husband."

Unbelievable, we had a regular Caitlyn Jenner on our hands.

He, she, stepped in and stopped at the view of me in the buff. "Oh my, my, my."

'Holy shit' would have been less threatening. My willy didn't like her staring at him. "Somehow I don't suspect you are here to talk about your manuscript."

Howard viewed the room. "It would appear I've come at a bad time."

He, she turned to leave when Littleton discovered his own nut sack and took charge. "You aren't going anywhere."

"Excuse me?" Howard turned, and her face didn't lend itself to debate. "Are you talking to me?"

"Yeah, you freak, I am."

"And who are you?" Howard, put her hands against her black skirt, her blouse pushed out by an ample chest. Those red pumps I wanted to see on Ebony didn't look so good on a figure with hairier legs than me. I did like the pearls though, nice touch of elegance.

"I'm Detective Littleton, and I have a few questions about your wife's death."

About fucking time your fat ass got around to the case.

"What would you like to know?"

Littleton dismissed me as a shield and approached Howard, gun drawn. "Where were you the day your wife was killed?"

"What are you suggesting, Detective?"

"Dr. Coleman said he heard her being fucked that day. Were you the mysterious guest in her office?"

"If you are suggesting I had a post divorce tryst with my wife, I can assure you that is most definitely impossible."

"And why is that?"

Howard hiked up her skirt and exposed her kooch.

"Oh Lord!" I brought up a little into my mouth. The room held a collective gasp. That pussy looked like Freddy Krueger on a bad day. I waved her to stop. "Put the dress down, Howard. If any crime has been committed, the doctor who did that to you should be arrested."

She massaged it. "She's beautiful."

I joined in on the questioning. "As much as you think that might be true, and clearly it is in the eye of the beholder, can we get back to the puzzle?"

Unaware that Howard could turn less attractive, my question brought an expression of disgust that didn't make her beautiful. She reached into her purse and pulled out a handgun. Why on earth Littleton didn't shoot her is beyond me, but for the third time that morning, he stood toe to toe in a standoff.

"Smooth move, Littleton."

"How was I supposed to know this clown was drawing a gun?"

"This clown killed his wife and cut her head off."

Howard protested. "I did not."

Being naked and animated in an interrogation led to me swing like a pendulum and a focus issue for the broad. I had to remind Howard to look at my face. "Pay attention." I continued. "Don said he heard heavy steps and a high feminine voice. That describes you, Howard."

Howard wiped a tear. "I didn't say I wasn't there, I said I didn't kill her."

"Who did?"

Howard sighed. "It wasn't supposed to go down like that." She remained squared-off with Littleton. "We went to Stella's office, and he fucked her. I couldn't believe it. I never knew he had been having an affair with her, he was having one with me."

More bile in my throat. Stella was bad enough, but an affair with Howard? Wow, that had to be one sick fuck. "Who?"

"She freaked, and he shot her. I didn't want that."

"Who?"

"Then we went to your office and someone was here. I panicked and guess I didn't know my own strength."

"What about Eddie?"

"Eddie?"

"The maintenance man."

"He came along when we were disposing of bodies. I led him upstairs to the roof. The plan was to toss him off, but he ran and tripped and impaled himself. He screamed and screamed, and I was instructed to stop him. So I did."

Littleton took over. "Who were you with?"

Howard fixed on Hal. "Who is that?"

The question was rhetorical. She lowered her gun and moved past us to the corpse. "No!" she plopped onto her butt and pulled Hal's head to her lap. "Oh, baby, please don't be dead."

The room closed in and circled the two on the ground, Howard wailing for the dead man in her lap.

Littleton broke the ice. "Am I in a circus?" He aimed his gun at Howard. "Get the fuck up, you spastic."

"Leave her alone." Richelle had a little of me in her.

"Unless you want me to shoot you, shut the fuck up, you little cunt."

Don stood from behind us, and Littleton turned and fired. Don went down in a heap.

"You fucking dick. I stepped forward and Littleton discharged two rapid shots into my chest. I reeled backward and fell to floor. That jacket worked but I couldn't breathe. "Shit" pushed out in lost air.

My eyes misted, but I could make out Littleton standing over me. "Flak jacket? Nice." He bent over and put the barrel against my forehead. "Doesn't do much good against a head shot though."

I closed my eyes and the concussion of an explosion rang out over my head. Next thing I knew, gunfire zinged back and forth above me. Four feet from each other and Littleton couldn't hit Howard and Howard couldn't hit Littleton.

I hurt so bad all I could do was watch as Howard stood and charged Littleton. She had that fat fuck in her paws and choked the shit out of him while Littleton discharged his second gun into her. A loud crack and Littleton turned limp like a ragdoll. Howard fell to her knees, her silk white blouse a Rorschach of blood. She turned to me and asked "Are you okay?" She fell beside me. "So, if I die will you publish my work?"

I might have been shot, but I wasn't stupid. "Hell no."

"Why?"

"Because it's terrible. Death won't change that."

She coughed up blood and reached for my wiener.

"Don't do that."

"Just one touch, please."

"No."

"I just want to touch it."

Muffin and Dee nodded. "Dick, you should, it's really special."

Richelle agreed, "Let her, Dad."

The poet coffee-server added, "I'm writing a poem about it."

The kid with the black eyes chimed in, "I'd actually like to touch it myself. I say let her." His three friends agreed.

Charles stared, amazed.

Jamie offered, "I've touched it, it's wonderful." Her brother shook his head yes.

"Oh what the hell, but don't linger!"

She died with a death grip on my dick.

After prying her hand off my wiener, the group lifted me up, and I made my way to Don.

"Damn it, Don, what were you thinking?"

His eyes snapped open. "I wanted to help."

I grinned. "You're alive."

I could see a blood coming through his jacket. I lifted it and inside the bullet had grazed his chest after bouncing off something. I pulled it out and looked at it. "Why do you have a vaginal specula in your pocket? You're a foot doctor."

"Well, funny thing about that —"

"Never mind, I don't think I want to know. Looks like you earned your scar."

Don smiled. "Yeah, I guess I did."

Still, he's a pussy.

"Can someone get me some pants?"

Chapter 52

That's how my five fucking days went. I'm bruised from two bullets hitting me in the chest, but worse, my heart is kind of bruised from a Nubian princess, and if that doesn't take the cake, one of L.A.'s finest is now pulling me over.

Son of a bitch.

I adjust my mirror and hide my face. I have no idea just how bad this is going to get but I'm prepared for a swarm of cops to descend upon me like locust. I turn the car off, close my eyes, and tilt my thoughts against the head rest. I can hear the click of shoes on pavement but just don't have the desire to see another cop.

"Going somewhere in a hurry?"

I open one eye and leaning through my window, Ebony slides a pair of new shades down.

Too tired to argue, I resume resting. "Are you going to shoot me too?"

Ebony puts her forearms on my door. "No, I went home this morning and emptied out my bank account so I could buy these sunglasses. Later today, I'm quitting the police force. Figure I don't need the job anymore."

I'm watching the inside of my eyelids. "Oh yeah, you come into some money?"

"No, but my new boyfriend did."

I slide my lids open and Ebony leans further in, close enough to rub noses with me. "Oh yeah?"

"I figure we might live on a boat, and I'd need these shades." She tosses a manila envelope in the car. "That is unless you found someone else?" Those luscious lips find mine and she kisses me.

My wiener gets hard.

randall 'Jay' andrews lives in Southern California with his wife and sons. He's worked as a writer for his adult life and has several titles prior to Five Days.

He can be found at www.jacolpublishing.com

He is also in the pages of Writers World on facebook, as well as randall andrews editing.